The Infinite Mystery of Being

Decima Wraxall

The Infinite Mystery of Being

The Infinite Mystery of Being
ISBN 978 1 76109 581 8
Copyright © text Decima Wraxall 2023
Cover image: Melissa Wraxall

First published 2023 by
GINNINDERRA PRESS
PO Box 3461 Port Adelaide 5015
www.ginninderrapress.com.au

Contents

Lost

Timing was vital. They should arrive just before dark – otherwise Connie might guess the danger. He wasn't about to swap one sort of prison for another. A tragic accident. What could be simpler?

Henry Rogers had traced the distance to the edge of Mount Danger a hundred times. It was imperative to know exactly how many steps were needed before a victim would tumble over that sheer drop. It took months of planning.

Even so, Henry had failed to take one thing into account. Fog. It came up quickly in these parts, making the terrain look entirely different. This morning, there hadn't been a cloud in the sky.

He had said, 'It's the perfect day for an outing. Why not join me?'

Connie had seemed pleased. She often complained he didn't invite her out.

The Ford stalled as planned. He'd made a pretext of trying to start it again. The engine didn't even splutter.

'Drat. Forgot to fill her up.'

'Oh, you fool. How could anyone forget to buy petrol? Now we're stuck here, miles from anywhere.'

He turned, hiding a little smile. Felt the spanner in his jacket. 'We'll borrow some. There's a farmhouse.'

'Where?'

'Further along. I often take walks here.'

She shuddered. 'I don't like this place. I'll stay in the car until someone happens along.'

'This road is rarely used. Not a tyre mark in sight,' he said. 'But feel free to relax here while I…' He pretended to leave. Henry guessed she'd follow, scared of being alone in the bush.

The ark-ark-ark of a crow echoed somewhere in the murk.

'What was that?' Connie's kilos wobbled as she made to join him.

They set off along a faint track. She lagged behind. He frequently stopped, allowing her to catch up.

Connie gasped for breath. 'We could be heading anywhere. Let's stick to the road.'

'This is a short cut, Precious.'

'Another of your mess-ups. Daddy was right: I never should have married you.'

Henry's face didn't move a muscle. He's heard it all before.

'You fool… Can't…even organise…a trip to the country.' Every noise made Connie groan. 'What were you thinking? Bringing me to this horrible place.'

'I just wanted to please you.'

'Huh!' Her sudden wail of panic. 'We're lost. This is the second time we've passed those yellow everlasting daisies.'

Henry feared she was right. A sinking feeling. 'Once we reach the plateau, it'll be easy to see…'

'Where we are? In this fog? You must be joking.'

Somewhere in the gloom, a kookaburra laughed.

Connie moaned anew. 'To think I've wasted my life on the likes of you.'

Henry thought, not for much longer, my love. Once, long ago, he'd found her pretty. Of course, there had been times of happiness, in the early days. Shared laughter, before he became the butt of her scorn. He'd abandoned his dreams, one by one.

A trip? Connie had preferred an expensive makeover of their cottage. Not that it needed any changes.

An evening college course to improve his education and job prospects? He could still hear her scornful laughter. 'Waste of time and money.' Yet she made him feel less than a man for his modest salary.

Henry had prided himself on bearing her jibes in stoic silence. Even when they stung like a lash. But when she froze out the last of his friends, something snapped. I ought to have left long ago, he thought. Yet far from ready to abandon his comfortable home for some cheap, rented flat. Or to split their assets when she hadn't contributed a penny. I worked hard to pay off the darned mortgage. Divorce wasn't an option. Connie would find some clever lawyer – no, no, no. He wasn't about to see her take the cream of everything.

On one of his solitary bushwalks, Henry had hatched his plan. Since then, he had thought of little else. He had carried out experiments to discover how far he could drive after the fuel gauge showed empty. The prospect of freedom tantalised him.

Connie took the lead. Pushed by some superhuman energy, she plunged forward in her blue crimplene slacks. Crunched through the undergrowth. Stumbled against old logs. Slid on damp rocks. Stopped frequently to berate him, gasping for air, red and perspiring. He almost smiled over her harsh words.

A wait-a-while vine ripped through the thin fabric of her blouse. 'Ouch,' she wailed, 'Ouch! I'm hurt.'

'A small cut.' Henry wiped away the blood with his clean handkerchief, beautifully ironed. 'Let's keep moving.'

'Oh,' she whimpered. 'It's painful.'

'Best press on. Light's going fast.' Familiar landmarks made him almost certain they were heading in the right direction.

Connie stifled sobs. 'You idiot. Getting us into this.' She clawed at a small shrub, edging forward.

The fog partially cleared for a moment. Enough for Henry to see that she had reached the summit. Damn. He was meant to be there first. Trust Connie to take the lead. His breath came in painful gasps, a pounding in his ears, a cough clawed at his chest. He thought, must have been out of my mind to dream up this crazy scheme. Divorce? Probably the only way out. He felt relieved in a funny sort of way.

Buffeted by strong winds, Connie seemed to be having trouble keeping herself upright. 'Hurry along, Henry.'

He saw her take a step forward. Caught by a stronger gust, she teetered, grasping for non-existent handholds. Both her arms held out, the beginning of a plunge, he realised. Her scream of terror stirred the hairs on the back of his neck.

'Help me! H-e-n-r-y...'

Time slowed. Her scream seemed to last forever.

Fog and the angle of her fall stole Connie from his sight. Even after her cries had faded, muffled by the sound of falling rocks, they continued in his head. He shuddered. A rush of relief. *It's over, thank God. And I didn't have to do a thing.*

In the shrieking gusts of wind, he suddenly felt numb. Another few steps and he would have joined her.

Darkness caught him by surprise. The edge of that precipice loomed terrifyingly close. He felt almost scared of breathing. Afraid to budge, not even to find some sort of shelter. If only he'd brought a torch, and matches to make a fire.

Thank goodness Connie had made him wear his old leather jacket. Henry eased himself into a horizontal position against a damp log. Limited protection, half-awake through that long and wretched night. Would it ever end? Henry's throat felt as if it had been lacerated with broken glass. He'd ask Connie to make him some of her famous chicken soup. She'd tuck him up in bed with a hot-water bottle. Then he remembered. Suffering the pangs of a small boy who'd lost his mother.

Morning brought a clear brightness. Rigid with cold, teeth jittering, Henry struggled to move, stiff in his lower limbs. Light-headed, he shuddered back from the sight of something blue sprawled on the rocks far, far below.

Henry closed his eyes. He felt strange and disorientated.

Shivering, he forced his frozen legs to move, stumbling over stones and tussocks. Now it was him stopping to catch his breath, racked by coughing. At last he located the hollow tree with the petrol container. Hiding the empty can, he drove off. It took twice his usual concentration to manage the morning traffic. An accident, that's all he needed to say.

At the police station, he leant on the reception desk. He had no reason to feel nervous. It could happen to anyone.

The desk officer eyed his unkempt appearance, his pallor. 'Good God, man. What's up?'

'My wife, Connie…lost last evening on Mount Danger.'

The room spun.

Someone helped him onto a chair. With the greatest effort, Henry told of Connie being separated in the fog.

In a flurry of orders, they began to organise a search. 'Must be there.'

He tried to stand, would have fallen if they hadn't caught him. Henry was dimly aware of an ambulance siren.

In the week to follow, he had a comforting sensation of soft voices and caring hands. Guessing it was day by the quilt. Finally, he fully regained consciousness. The nurse said he'd been very ill with pneumonia.

'Did I…uh…talk?'

She laughed. 'You rambled a lot. We couldn't make much sense of it.'

Henry coughed. 'And…my wife…has she…is she…?'

The nurse avoided his eyes. 'Speak to your doctor.'

The intern was young. He looked ill-at-ease, clearly a novice at dealing with tragedy. 'Bad news, I'm afraid. Your wife…'

'She didn't survive the fall?' The second Henry spoke the words, he longed to bite them back.

The doctor looked at him strangely. 'No.'

Henry cried. He guessed it was expected of him.

'When…if you're…uh…up to it, the police want an interview.'

Henry grabbed a tissue and wiped his eyes. 'Police? Of course. Well, I'd better see them, hadn't I?'

The doctor scanned his face. 'Do you feel well enough?'

'Yes, yes. I'd prefer to get it over with.' Henry sat up against the freshly plumped pillows. Ready to savour the role of bereaved husband.

'Mr Rogers? I'm Detective Sergeant Mason and this is Detetective Constable Williams.'

Before starting the interview, they set up a tape recorder, warned him that anything he said…

His mind drifted. He'd heard it so many times on police shows.

'You're entitled to legal representation,' one of them said. It all seemed horribly formal.

'I'm sure that won't be necessary.'

The officer called Mason showed him a metal object. 'For the tape, I'm showing exhibit A… Recognise this?'

'Yes. That's my spanner,' Henry said wearily.

'You know where this was found?'

'In my car, I suppose.' Suddenly, he recalled the last time he'd seen it. The expressions on their faces made him afraid. 'Look, officer, it must have fallen from my jacket while I was asleep.'

They exchanged glances. 'So you admit carrying a concealed weapon?'

'Surely you don't think…'

'Shall we stop playing games? Your wife was found with a fractured skull and numerous other injuries.'

Henry began to tremble. 'I wasn't even near Connie when she fell.'

'So you've wasted our time pretending your wife was lost? What really happened?'

'It was an accident, officer. Caught by a gust of wind…'

'I say that after attacking your wife, you cleaned the weapon, concealing it under a log above the cliffs at Mount Danger. Exhibit B, for the tape. This handkerchief came from your pocket, Mr Rogers. It's yours?'

Henry gave it a cursory glance. 'Yes.'

'Forensic have identified your wife's blood group.'

'Connie cut her arm. I wiped away the blood.'

'You also claimed to have run out of petrol, Mr Rogers. Exhibit C. Can you explain this empty petrol container? You hid it, did you not?'

Henry gulped.

'Do you always carry a spare just in case? Or was this a special occasion?' The interviewing officer raised his eyebrows. 'You attempted to cross out your initials. But with modern imaging techniques, evidence can't easily be obliterated.'

Henry squirmed. This has gone terribly, terribly wrong, he thought. I'm innocent.

'Henry Archibald Rogers,' the officer went on, 'I'm charging you with first-degree murder. I say you struck the said Amelia Constance Rogers with this spanner, then pushed her body over the cliff.'

Henry turned to ice. 'No, no – you've got it all wrong. I was nowhere near my wife when she fell.'

'You must admit, Mr Rogers, the evidence is overwhelming. What have you to say?'

'Evidence?' Henry's head throbbed. If only Connie were here to tell him what to do. He knew what she'd say. Get a good brief, you fool.

The Broken Windmill

The ceiling fan creaked and groaned. Patients coughed. My brother Eric sat high against the pillows, face grey. Red-striped pyjamas hung on his gaunt frame, sizes too large.

I whispered hello, a lump in my throat. Touched by his drowsy greeting. Wife Peppie pecked him on his cheek, and groped for a chair.

Eric stabbed the morphine driver. Dozed.

My father wore a stoic expression. Three days had passed since the operation. Three days of fear and doubt. Three days without a word from the surgeon. His son's illness seemed one blow too many, following the recent loss of his beloved wife, Genn.

IV fluid swelled into translucent droplets. Plop, plop, plop.

Eric's eyes flicked open.

Dad seized the opportunity. 'Have you seen the doctor?'

The rasp of our patient's voice. 'Not yet.' Eric's eyelids drooped. He drifted off.

Late that afternoon, my brother woke with a start. 'Thought you'd all be gone by now… Road's risky in darkness.'

Dad swallowed. 'We're just leaving, son.'

My turn for a hug. I could count every rib.

Peppie gave Eric a cheek-peck. He squeezed her hand.

The balm of a warm breeze caressed my face. I felt relieved to escape the odour of antiseptic and death.

Peppie took the wheel.My father folded his long legs into the front of the Holden. Click, clack. Me in the back.

The narrow road twisted around hillsides. Ravines on one side, steep incline on the other, shadowed with native oak.

Peppie screeched around corners. I grabbed for support.

Dad shot me an anxious glance. Worried, too. He said, 'Slow down a bit, Peppie. Never know who might be on the wrong side of the road at the next corner.'

She eased back on the gas. I breathed again. A convoy of army truck roared by. The final vehicle put us into the gutter. The driver laughed on his way.

Dad muttered, 'Darn fool.'

Little farms yelped with guard dogs. A gaunt donkey swished its tail. In one drought-brown valley, a windmill's broken blades hung motionless in the hot air. Oddly, it reminded me of Eric. Once, he, too, spun with every breeze.

A huge white cockatoo flapped to rest in a skeletal tree. Slanting light and its raucous cries, brought me answers I didn't want to know.

Should all go well with an operation, the surgeon emerges from the theatre, triumphant. 'Got it all, folks.' But when the only communication is silence? She would delay until a patient gained enough strength to hear bad news.

I pondered how long Eric might have? Six months? A year?

Later, I blurted out my fears to Dad.

He lifted stricken eyes. 'Dear God, I hope you're wrong.'

We made a second pilgrimage to the hospital. Dazzling sunshine, sombre mood. Black feathers squabbled in a grove of eucalypts. Ark-ark, they cried.

Dad shook his fist. 'Bloody crows.'

Eric greeted us with a smile. Wincing as he hauled himself up by the grab ring. His voice sounded stronger. 'I'm fine.'

A sign on the bed said, 'Nil By Mouth'.

The IV swelled into huge drops. He regurgitated bile into a sputum mug. Rinsed away acid with water from a foam tumbler. Sucked ice cubes. Stabbed the magic button on his morphine driver. Drifted off.

My unease pulsed with his every breath.

Dad sat in the nearby armchair. His pale hands trembled against the curve of his walking stick, one on top of the other.

At last, Eric blinked awake.

Dad broke the silence. 'Have you seen the doctor?'

'Yes.'

'What did he say?'

'Oh, he's quite pleased with me.'

Dad's puzzled glance met mine. He persisted. 'Were there any other spots?'

'Oh yes, Dad,' said Eric, amazingly cheerful. 'It's terminal.'

His triumphant tone sent a chill shivering down my spine. How typical of Eric to use the correct term, even *in extremis*.

Dad turned ashen. Two large tears rolled down his cheeks. He didn't wipe them away, oblivious in his shocked state.

Peppie blinked. A small red spot flamed on either cheek.

I choked at his words. Craving space to share my grief and sense of impending loss.

We dined at a little café in the mall. I gagged at the smell of old cooking oil.

Vulnerable and afraid. The glare of fluorescents disturbed me.

Dad and I picked at our salads.

Peppie tucked into her meal with gusto. By then, her whole face was ablaze. The high pitch of her voice confirmed her agitation. 'Doesn't look as if I'll be able to get the car air conditioner fixed today. Have to return it next week.'

Barely holding it together, I thought. The car was a safe topic that didn't risk emotions spilling into tears. Verbal communication was never her strong point. Why had I expected things to be different today?

Her marriage had been a troubled one. If Eric dared ask a relative or friend to dinner, Peppie made his life hell for the next weeks.

The lovely bride of yesteryear had packed on the kilos. Waddled around the house in a grimy shift, scaly feet in trodden-down slippers. Then came Peppie's weight loss, and smart new clothes. Confirming what I had already guessed.

Whispers had reached me of Eric's fling with an attractive jillaroo. Julia was a talented cattle worker. Full of fun and laughter. Adored by Eric's children. Nobody discussed her sudden departure. The little ones' curiosity was met by a stone wall of adult silence.

The one puzzle was why Dad had signed the property over to Eric. I pushed aside my half-finished meal. Families.

Back at the ward, staff avoided our eyes. It seemed the relatives of a dying man were invisible. Perhaps this sucker of ice with the morphine-dried mouth presented a sharp reminder of their own mortality?

In my day, nurses showed empathy and compassion – or was I getting old and grumpy? Still, I craved a pat on the shoulder, a hug. Aching to hear those age-old words, 'Must be difficult for you.'

That surreal afternoon drew towards its coda.

A nursing sister approached us. 'Would you like some tea?'

I offered to help. In the kitchen, I seized the opportunity. 'Dad's shocked by the news. Eric is more than a son – he's a mate.'

The nurse feigned deafness. She busied herself, arranging cups and saucers. Avoided my eyes. Voice sing-song. 'Make yourselves a cup of tea any time you like.'

I returned to Sydney. Glad to hear that Eric had left hospital. Hoping he might enjoy some quality moments with his family before...

My brother planned to celebrate their thirtieth wedding anniversary on the coast. I worried about such a journey, given his circumstances. Typical Eric, I thought. Determined not to let illness spoil this special weekend.

Given Peppie's penchant for speed, I pictured Eric clutching his suture line at every bump in the road.

Two hours into the journey, his distress reached crisis point. Peppie bypassed the motel and rushed him to casualty. Staff gave him morphine for his intolerable pain. Put up a blood transfusion.

Emergency surgery relieved the distress of a blocked intestine.

I visited on the third day. Apprehensive at finding Eric alone.

All my adult life, our conversations had been awkward. The way he sought to prove his intellectual superiority irritated me. But now Eric greeted me with a hug. His wide grin seemed at odds with the results from his latest scan: secondaries on his liver.

He relaxed against the lumpy pillow as if it were swansdown. 'Don't worry about me, sis,' he said, 'This is the best part of my life. For the first time ever, I can sit back and marvel at the moon and stars. See the buds open. Enjoy the scent of lilacs.'

A nurse brought back my big bunch of flowers, now in a crystal vase. The red roses and baby's breath were beautifully arranged. 'Don't they look lovely?'

'Thank you so much, nurse.'

'It's a pleasure.'

Eric looked delighted. 'Thanks, sis.'

Childhood memories flew back and forth.

Eric's eyes grew dreamy. 'Remember how we explored the rolling hills and fields? Not so much as a pair of shoes.'

'And waded in the Hunter River? I loved the weeping willows with their halo of pink roots drifting in the current.'

He nodded. 'And I skipped stones across the water. We roamed everywhere with the freedom of mice.'

Towards the end of the afternoon, I gathered my things, fighting tears. If only this easy communication had happened earlier.

Eric glanced around, as if afraid of being overheard. 'Need your help, sis. Strictest confidence. Could you find out what became of Julia?'

I blinked.

Eric's voice surged with emotion. 'I've never loved anyone so much.'

Perfect love, I thought, unsullied by reality. 'Tell me.'

His eyes glowed. 'We rode out in the still pale mornings of winter, knee to knee, holding hands. My horse black, hers a bay. Mist steamed from the cold paddocks. Hooves cracked the ice above pools of water, the sound like breaking glass.'

In their laughing intimacy, everything must have seemed possible.

Clearly, Eric remained smitten, all those years later. 'I was ready to abandon everything.'

Tales of blazing rows with our mother astonished me. 'But...you were always the perfect son. Her favourite.'

His wry grin. 'Mum saw her dreams disappearing with my divorce. Threatened to sack Julia. I told her if she did that, I'd leave.'

I shook my head.

'What our parents called good sense prevailed. Julia packed her bags. Worst day of my life. If it hadn't been for my kids...'

'So that's why Dad signed over the property to you?'

A flicker of guilt crossed his pallid face. 'Some time later, Julia wrote to me, care of Mum. She worked at a roadhouse up north. Said she'd be there for twelve weeks. Enclosed a letter for me but...'

In a flash, I guessed. 'Mum didn't pass it on?'

'She kept it for six months.'

'You must've been furious.'

He nodded. 'About the time Julia wrote, a semi-trailer driver smashed his rig into her roadhouse.' He swallowed. 'People killed. Never knew whether Julia...'

'Was alive or dead?' I wiped away tears. 'All this time you've lived with that?'

His eyes shone with a feverish light. 'Peppie and I patched things up. But now...'

'You need to know?' I kissed him on the cheek. 'I'll do my best.'

I consulted the local directory. On the third call, an aunt gave me Julia's number.

I wondered how this young woman might react to an intrusion from the past. She hadn't married, but was in a relationship.

Julia's initial delight on hearing Eric's name turned to shock. I heard a catch to her voice. 'How long does he have?' She promised to write immediately.

Days later, I felt honoured to deliver her farewell letter.

Eric unfolded the document, hands trembling. 'I'll be... Well, I'll be... It's from her.' He read and reread the precious missive. Held the page against his chest as if she were in his arms.

I blinked back tears. Bade my brother farewell with a huge embrace. Knowing it might be forever. Surprised that his whole being emanated happiness. Guessing his love for Julia was enhanced by dire circumstances.

One morning not long afterwards, the call came from Dad. 'Darling... uh...'

My teeth began to chitter. 'Eric's gone?'

'Just before midnight.'

Eric had told Dad he would pass away that day.

The hairs stood up on the back of my neck.

'God knows how he knew.' Dad's voice was husky. 'So brave and accepting of his fate.'

In the pink veil of evening, I drove through the valleys toward our farm. Gripped by a sense of unreality. A wedge-shaped golden cloud hung low in the northern sky. The glowing beacon lead me on and on, mile after mile.

My hands tightened on the steering wheel.

A sign from Eric, I thought. His spirit lives on.

Button Boots

Our very own dance. A dream come true. I pictured faces shining in the lamp light. One of the guests might play the fiddle. Victor and I would join other kids, sliding around on the polished floor.

My parents met neighbours on horseback and invited them. Passed the word to locals, met by chance in town. Not everyone had a telephone in those days.

Daddy rubbed his big hands. 'It'll be a good night, Genn. Twenty guests have accepted so far.'

We kids pestered them for weeks. 'How many more sleeps?

'You'll know soon enough.' Dad chuckled. 'Run and play.'

I groaned. 'It's taking so long...'

'It is hard to wait.' Daddy grinned. 'I wager it'll be our best night ever.'

Mum pedalled away on her old Singer machine. Vivi and I danced in our new dresses. Mine, cotton, with scattered pink rosebuds, white Peter Pan collar and long sash. I loved it. Curly's frock was the same design, only hers had pink and white spots.

Three days to go. Mum pored over her recipe books.

I helped Mum bake pastry and biscuits. She made pies and cakes. The kitchen breathed with the fragrance of apples, cinnamon, nutmeg and other spices.

Daddy moved beds and cupboards to the far end of the front veranda, Whistling, he hid them under tarps. Victor helped move the smaller stuff.

We didn't guess what would happen next. We watched in amazement: our father slid out weatherboards between two medium-sized bedrooms. Our eyes widened at the appearance of one huge room. He applied beeswax to the boards. 'Go for it, kids.'

Victor and I slid back and forth on mats, gleefully exchanging glances. How the floor shone!

We busied ourselves making red and yellow paper chains. Daddy helped us to hang them around the room. He hung bunches of multi-coloured balloons.

His face one big grin. 'What do you reckon, folks?'

Mum said, 'Gosh. It does look good.'

It felt as if someone had waved a magic wand.

Daddy said, 'Best ballroom ever.'

Just one more sleep before the fun began.

The day of our party dawned bleak and overcast. Dark skies failed to dampen my high spirits. I drooled at the whiff of baking lamb. Roast potatoes and pumpkin added to the tantalising aromas. Beans were ready for a quick boil on the stove.

Late that afternoon, Mum dunked my little sister Curly in the round tin tub. Then it was my turn. She scrubbed each from us from head to toe, using a washer and Pears soap. She gave special attention to my neck and ears. Ouch! The transparent tablets reminded me of amber sap which exuded from wattle trees.

I stepped out into a soapy pool of water. Towelled my dripping body. 'How much longer?'

'They'll all be here in no time. Hurry and get dressed.'

Mum helped me on with my button boots. I must have been among the last little girls to wear such archaic footwear.

She used a special hook to fasten the tiny black buttons. Her sigh. 'Goodness, they're almost worn out.'

I felt a stab of sadness: they were my favourites.

Victor was next in the tub.

I fancy our parents added more hot water to improve the grey bath water.

Dusk drizzled into sodden darkness.

Daddy sighed. 'I'm glad it's not a downpour.'

Mum wore a new green dress. Glass beads glittered at her throat, hair swept up. She had never looked happier.

Daddy whistled, giving her a hug. 'You'll be the belle of the ball.'

She blushed. 'Get off with you.'

Victor declared, 'It's seven o'clock.'

I envied him telling the time. Our friends should arrive at any moment.

Time dragged. Mum gave us children our meals. She helped Vivi with hers. The lamb was tender and delicious. Gravy was just the way I liked it, brown and yummy. I bit into a baked potato, floury in the middle. Perfect apple pie...

Victor wiped his lips. 'Seven thirty.'

Daddy eased his tie. Usually, he only wore one to town.

My little sister's eyes kept closing.

Mum said, 'It's bedtime, little one.'

She stifled a yawn. 'No, Mumma.'

'Say goodnight, dear.'

'Ni-ni, Dadda.'

We kissed her.

Mum tucked Curly into bed. I fancy she fell asleep the moment her blonde mop touched the pillow.

Mum gave a contented sigh. 'Not a peep out of her, thank goodness.'

Daddy began to pace. 'What can be keeping them?'

Mum swallowed. 'It's a pity Cousin Charlie and Poppy are away.'

He nodded. 'Yep. They'd have been here by now, no mistake.'

I ached for their company. Charlie called me 'Blondie'. Sometimes he tickled me until I shrieked for mercy, laughing nonetheless. We liked Poppy's merry eyes and jokes, too.

Eight p.m. came...and went. Trapped by heavy silence, I squirmed. Longing for the trot of horses and the creak of buggies.

Victor joined Daddy in pacing. Sombre and serious, hands behind his back. 'Eight thirty. Where are they?'

The sparkle had left Mum's eyes. 'Oh, do be quiet.' Saying to nobody in particular, a break in her voice, 'Surely they haven't forgotten?'

Daddy studied his work-roughened hands.

Victor chimed in, 'Nine o'clock.'

Mum glared. 'Do be quiet.'

I strained my eyes and ears. Wiping away the sting of tears. Oh, where were they? I sucked the ends of my sash. It made me feel better.

The squeak of metal wheels on gravel. Our dogs barked. The stamp of hooves.

I danced my happiness.

Daddy beamed. 'Someone's arrived.'

Mum grabbed the damp ends of my sash. 'Stop that at once, Dessie. You're such a baby.'

She tied the bow so tightly I could hardly breathe, slapping my leg. It stung, but I didn't cry.

A buggy drew up outside.

The dark shape of a man. He attached the reins to a wire hook on the fence. 'Sorry we're late,' said Mr Spencer.

Daddy held up an umbrella. In the yellowish illumination from a hurricane lamp, Mr Spencer helped his wife alight.

Drops of water dripped from oilskin coats.

Daddy hung them on the veranda pegs. Pumped his friend's hand. 'No problem at all, Reg. Glad you could make it.'

Mrs Spencer stepped inside. Pecked Mum on the cheek, kissed me. I loved her lavender perfume.

She glanced around in surprise. 'Oh! We're the first… My! You have gone to a lot of trouble, Genn. And Joly's made this into one big room. What a wonderful idea.'

Mum gave a pleased smile.

Daddy said, 'What's your poison?'

I giggled, and guessed what he was asking.

The ladies settled for a shandy, the men took beer. Daddy poured Vance and me lemonade.

In the flickering lamplight, Victor wound up our His Master's Voice gramophone. Old-time waltzes like 'After the Ball' and 'If you were the Only Girl In the World' quavered from the machine. Adults took turns around the floor.

Mr Spencer winked. 'C'mon, Blondie. Have this one with me.'

I blushed.

He held out his arms. Almost as tall as Daddy, Mr Spencer's hair bore same golden red hue. He whirled me around the room. I felt giddy, but liked his smile.

The night was silent. Now and then a chorus of barking broke the stillness. Mr Spencer's horse stamped, whinnied.

I half-closed my eyes. Pretending I could see a room full of whirling couples. Hear the laughter and chatter from all of my parents' friends. How sad that they had missed our dance.

Adults enjoyed a late supper at a table groaning with food.

I tried a biscuit. It went down in lumps.

A flush had crept to Mum's cheeks. 'Seconds of apple pie, anyone? Cake?'

My body drooped. I fought to stay awake.

The Spencers departed, laden with cakes, slices, pies...

Mum gazed at all the uneaten food. 'Enough left to feed an army. Why do people promise to come?'

Daddy gulped. 'If the weather hadn't been so darn miserable...'

She stamped. 'A sprinkle of rain? Don't make excuses for them.' Moisture sparkled in her blue eyes. 'It's damn bad manners to say they'll attend. Then not turn up.'

Daddy sighed. 'Maybe you're right.'

That dance heralded their first, and last, attempt at formal entertaining.

The Inheritance

Ivy Cramp settled her bulky frame into a tourist class seat on the 747. She wiped her eyes.

'Do you think you're doing the right thing, Mum?' Dolly had asked at Heathrow.

'I say. It's rather too late for that question.' Son-in-law Basil brushed back a thatch of dark hair, speckled with grey. He wore a heavy overcoat against the cold. His moustache had looked stiff and half-frozen.

Cedric and Ian had clung to her. 'Don't go, Gran.'

What madness had possessed her to make this hateful journey to the Antipodes? Leaving her family. Giving up her cosy little garden flat – she had loathed letting that go.

Still, Dolly could mind her good things. 'I'll soon be home with the loot,' she said in an odd, cheerless voice.

'What's the loot, Gran?' asked Ian.

The adults had laughed.

Ivy whispered, 'Little pigs.'

'Never you mind, sweetie,' said Dolly. 'Gran just means she'll be back with lots of goodies.'

'And the money?' asked Cedric.

In the heavy silence, adults exchanged glances.

Dolly told the boys to give Gran another kiss. 'It's time for her to board the plane.'

Ivy struggled to attach the seat belt. The balding man beside her demonstrated how to fasten it. 'Ta. That's ever so kind,' she said, adding loudly, 'It's my first flight.' She laughed to hide her anxiety. How silly to be afraid. Hadn't she survived the Blitz? It'll be worth it, she mused, Never regret anything I do.

'Ted's the name,' said her neighbour. 'Holiday, is it?'

'Ivy. Ivy Cramp.' She gulped. 'I'm emigrating. My brother-in-law is terribly ill… Dying, in fact.'

'Sorry to hear that, Ivy. And you plan to care for him?'

She nodded.

'Considerate, I must say. But what about…after?'

'Well, my daughter Dolly, and her family, plan to immigrate. When everything's settled in the UK.'

'Good luck, then. Best country in the world, Australia, even if I do say so meself.'

Lights blinked. Warning bells reminded them to fasten seat belts. The stop smoking sign went on. Ivy's feet clamped against the floor. Luggage lines and trucks passed. The plane taxied along the runway, changed direction, gathered speed.

'Keep your head up as we take off, Ivy. Stops a nasty pain in the ears, to do with pressure,' said Ted.

Ivy closed her eyes, rigid with fear. The big motors whined up to full throttle. What if the thing crashed? Never to see her little boys again?

'They'll have parachutes, Gran,' five-year-old Ian had said.

'Don't be silly,' Cedric laughed. He was nearly eight. 'The cabins are pressurised.'

Ivy would have felt a lot safer had there been a parachute stashed under her seat. Serve her right if something ghastly happened, never having ventured beyond London.

They soared into the sky. She found it hard to believe. Everything still felt safe and solid. The 747 dipped one wing and changed course. Levelled out. The Thames disappeared below the clouds. Motors settled into a steady hum.

Ivy shifted in her seat. Fleecy clouds, far below, drifted past the small window. It was quite pleasant, this flying. How I'll treat the boys when I come home, she thought. Outings, all the toys they desire from Hamleys. So what if she needed to repay the Australian government for her airline ticket?

She closed her eyes. Recalled the tough time after the death of her husband, Reg. She'd scrubbed other people's floors. Given second-hand clothing new identities with her old Singer machine. Raised and educated Dolly.

Jack and his late wife Bessie had been generous. She'd lost count of the food parcels they sent during the war. Items Britishers hadn't seen for ages. Things they would never have been able to afford.

She had often joked with Basil and Dolly about their rich uncle. Jack had made it plain that they stood to inherit everything. The catch was they must immigrate: none of them had had any desire to do so. Then came the death of poor Bessie.

Jack's letters told of his loneliness, begging Ivy to come. 'There's ample room in my lovely brick home for all of you,' he said. 'A large sunny yard. Lots of fresh air for active, growing lads.'

Ivy had responded with sympathetic letters. Cautious, as ever. Wishing that she could get her hands on the money without the need to leave England.

His barely decipherable handwriting raised questions. 'Had a very bad turn last week…didn't think I'd make it…they had to fetch the doctor twice.'

'Maybe I should go.' Ivy's eyes glittered. 'He seems a lot worse.'

'It's not worth it, Mum. These old boys with bad hearts can go on for years.'

Ivy couldn't stop dreaming. Once they received that inheritance, their troubles would be over.

The content of Jack's letters became even more tantalising. 'The doctor's very worried about my ticker… I spent a couple of weeks in hospital…home but feel terribly weak… Confined to the house for months. If it wasn't for my neighbours doing the shopping and cooking… Not the same as having family nearby. Got the feeling I won't be around much longer.'

Letters arrived from the neighbour.

'What did I tell you, Dolly?' Ivy couldn't hide her excitement. 'Jack's so frail he can't write. I'll go. Suppose some stranger got everything?' She dashed off a response. 'I'll come immediately arrangements are completed with Immigration. Give you care for life.'

Dolly giggled. 'You mean his life, not yours.'

Ivy looked over the top of her spectacles. 'Exactly,' she said. 'How does this bit sound: Dolly has always longed to live in Australia. She and Basil think it will be wonderful for the boys. They'll join us when their house is sold.'

Dolly wiped tears of mirth from her eyes.

'I shall be suitably distraught when he snuffs it, of course.' Ivy grinned. 'No need to be insensitive about these things.'

The Australian immigration people had proved difficult. But they took into account the perilous state of Jack's health. Learning that the whole family planned to join her, they finally gave consent.

Ivy chuckled. She recalled the triumph with which she had waved that letter. 'We fooled them!'

They all laughed.

Basil sniggered. 'So it's to be the Rainbow Flight Down Under.'

'And I'll be back with our pot of gold. I'm not about to let a rich relative out of the bag when he's ready to drop off the limb, if you get my drift.'

Dolly chortled. 'When he drops off the limb, Mum, he'll be in the bag.'

How she and Dolly had laughed as they packed two crates of surplus items from their respective homes. A Victorian tea trolley (I shall buy myself one of those super chromium and glass ones when I come home}. Her pre-war sewing machine (she never used it now), a folding clothesline (Ivy had a dryer), worn bed linen, musty fabric bought years ago, an old coat…

Ivy shook her head. 'What a shame paying good money on having these crates made, and cartage paid on this junk.'

'It must look as if you intend to stay, Mum. Jack would be suspicious if you arrived with only one suitcase. My friend who's organising passage of your goods will keep them in storage for a while. You'll be home before they leave Southampton.'

Ivy shifted into a more comfortable position, aching all over. Halfway round the world. The idea was more glamorous than the reality. Homesickness swept over her. How she'd miss them all. Even the Larsons who she did for on Thursdays, their sweet little girls… She wiped her eyes. Never mind, in a month or so she'd be back.

The lights were dimmed. She heard Ted's soft snore. Maybe that was why she couldn't sleep. A myriad of conflicting images and doubts crowded into her mind. For the hundredth time, she patted the battered old handbag. It bulged with photos of her family, her passport, the airline ticket.

One transit lounge resembled another. The changing time zones completely at variance with one's body clock. A farrago of bright lights and foreign faces at Singapore made Ivy feel nervous. She was glad to get back on the plane. Only a few more hours and it would be fait accompli.

Miss Evelyn Smythe had groaned inwardly. The social worker frowned when she inspected the red-brick cottage. Jerry-built after the First World War for returning heroes, it was Spartan, both inside and out. An outmoded kitchen and bathroom. No laundry. Two power points served the whole house. Power cords snaked from one room to another, attached to the refrigerator, tiny heater and black and white TV. Outside, the small yard was treeless and bare. A few shrubs struggled to survive.

It's a fantasy, she thought. A sister-in-law in England he hasn't seen in forty years. Offering to take care of him in his remaining days. She eyed the proud, white-haired old man. Said gently, 'It wouldn't work, Mr Tipper. She'd make you feel a stranger in your own home.'

Jack eyed her belligerently. His brown eyes flashed with anger. Who was this sour old maid telling him how to run his affairs. 'I'm used to being the boss in this house. What do you take me for? A fool?'

'Of course not.'

'I was in the services, you know. Navy. Nobody pushes Jack Tipper around. I may be a sick man but I can handle my own affairs.'

Miss Smythe felt perplexed. She admired the feisty old chap. Wanting to avoid causing distress. Yet she'd come to tell him that his proposal was impossible.

She faced these harsh realities every day. It was never easy, dashing their hopes. She hesitated, frowning. 'This…Ivy…is planning to come alone, you said? A woman in her sixties?' Her voice was deliberately cold and businesslike. 'My department doesn't look kindly on the immigration of elderly women – or men for that matter.' She gathered up her papers with an air of finality. 'It might be different if the family were coming at the same time.'

'But, I've told you…look.' He thrust a bundle of letters towards her. 'Dolly and Basil are very keen to immigrate. Soon's the house is sold.'

'How many boys are there?'

'Two. Cedric and Ian. Delightful kids. Look at their photos. Bessie and I always regarded them as our own.' He brushed aside something that looked suspiciously like a tear.

'It would be terribly cramped,' she said doubtfully, 'with only two bedrooms.'

'No problem. The boys can sleep on the veranda. I'll doss down here.'

She glanced at the tiny front veranda. 'With you here in the lounge room? Are you sure the family would be happy living like that?'

'Oh, it's only until they find a place of their own.'

'Mr Tipper, I fear that almost total strangers would have neither tolerance nor respect for your idiosyncrasies.' Persuasion, impatience, a hint of anger – nothing changed his mind. What a character, she thought.

He stood a his full height of five foot five. 'Ivy plans to come as soon as I give the word.'

She hesitated. 'I can't promise anything but my report will be filed immediately.'

'How long will it take?'

She laughed. 'Classified urgent.' Against her better judgement, Miss Smythe had decided to recommend that approval be given.

Driving away, she saw the little man silhouetted in the doorway. Surprisingly straight and strong for eighty-three, despite his many illnesses. Men of that calibre had made loss of the First World War unthinkable.

Jack watched her go. He had tried to explain the devastating months after Bessie died. It felt as if part of his own body had been ripped away. 'When we died,' he said, then corrected himself.

After sixty years of marriage, the loss was incalculable. Dark days stretched on and on. He hadn't cared what happened to him. Could barely bring himself to eat. It was only his navy training which ensured a strict adherence to the tenets of his life: A daily shower and shave, change of undies, house spotlessly clean.

But now, with firm plans for the arrival of Ivy, the clouds of gloom lifted. He had no reason to sit around feeling sorry for himself. He must get fit. Jack started doing long-abandoned exercises. Swung his arms around, massaged his legs. Did a lot of deep breathing.

At first, Jack forced himself to eat. But soon, his meals became enjoyable, rather than a chore. The first attempt in ages, he walked up the street. Rested twice on the way, the same coming back. A couple of Anginine. popped under his tongue, made it possible.

The letter of approval came from the Department of Immigration.

Jack shouted, 'Eureka.' He picked up the photo of his beloved Jessie. 'Don't worry, darlin', he whispered, 'everything will be proper and above board. I'll look after Ivy and make sure folks don't talk.'

The doctor visited. Pleased when he checked Jack over. 'Amazing how you've picked up since I saw you last. You've even put on weight.'

'My sister-in-law is coming to care for me,' said Jack. 'She's only young – in her sixties. Wouldn't like her to be tied down by an invalid. Want to show her around.'

'Excellent. Don't overdo things, though.' The doctor put his stethoscope into his bag. Showed Jack where to sign the bulk billing form.

At last came the Big Day. Jack was up at five a.m. doing his exercises. He made sure the house bore no trace of dust or disarray. He had shopped the previous day. Hadn't felt so healthy in years. Took an Anginine, just in case.

Jack wouldn't hear of a neighbour driving him to Mascot Airport. He caught a cab. One group of new arrivals after another emerged into the arrivals hall. He leant forward with growing impatience. Stamped his feet, ready to greet his sister-in-law.

Suddenly he spied Ivy. He would have recognised her anywhere. Tall, angular, big, loose overcoat. It was a surprise, though, to see the grey hair.

Ivy hesitated, blinking. Somehow, she'd have to find a taxi to her brother-in-law's place. She scrabbled for his address in her handbag.

Jack stood up straight, almost tall, despite his small stature. 'Ivy,' he called in a military sort of voice.

She looked around. Gaped. Not even a walking stick, she thought. What have I gotten myself into? Her head spun. She lost her grip on the trolley. Slid noiselessly to the floor.

'Stand back, everyone. Give the lady air,' said Jack. 'I've done first aid. Navy man meself.' He felt for her pulse, loosened the blouse neck button.

An official arrived with what looked like resuscitation equipment.

Ivy stirred. Opened her eyes. Someone helped her drink from a glass of water. Drowning in shock, she grabbed a life raft, her old handbag.

Horsewhipped

What better name for a fine black mare than Beauty?

Mum, the rider, towered above my father. Desperation in her voice, 'Aren't you ever going to give it up?'

Dad swayed below her. Over six feet six in his hobnailed boots, clutching a bottle of rum. He had stumbled around for over a week in the throes of his latest bender. The days had long gone when his lapses ended quickly. This one had come to stay. It made me feel helpless and angry.

I guess Mum felt the same. That day, something snapped. She flayed him with a whip. Screams of outrage rained down with every lash.

Horror in slow motion. I tried to blink it away. But her words echoed across our home valley.

Daddy stood in silence. Accepting every blow, as if he deserved them all.

Riveted to the spot, I dared not intervene. Suppose she turned on me?

An anguished shout came from behind me. My kid sister, Vivi. 'No, no, Mum! Stop!' Tears streamed down her face.

I fancy she recalled the many strappings suffered at her mother's hand.

Mum's whip hand hesitated in mid-flight. I didn't know if she'd come to her senses, or if Vivi would be her next victim.

A shake of her head. Her shout, 'Mind your own bloody business.' She wheeled Beauty, and cantered away.

Only then did I notice my kid brother, Druce. Ashen-faced. Desolate. He turned and slunk into the house. Shaken, I made to follow. Fearing the harm it might bring to a little boy watching his father humiliated in such a fashion.

Daddy blamed everything but alcohol for his problems. A sickly odour of booze exuded from every pore. He mumbled, 'Dessie, I often think man would be better off dead.'

I shivered. 'Don't say that, Daddy.'

Weapons in the house made it more than an idle threat. And now our mum had reached breaking point.

Memory of Dad's lashing lingered, an open wound. Leaving me heavy with shame, bubbling just under the surface.. Silence made it seem worse. Society regarded alcoholism as moral weakness. I dreaded the thought of our problem on the lips of people we knew. Little knowing that the story must have crept away long ago. Tendrils of a noxious vine, spreading from farmhouse to farmhouse, as these things do.

Two weeks' addiction stretched into three. And counting. Dad prowled the house, grey-faced. Searching for something – anything – to drink. Every bottle had been drained, even the medicinal sherry. His hands shook. He squeezed the empties a second time. Gaining a few drops of whisky, adding minuscule amounts of sherry and brandy. He could scarcely lift the glass to his lips.

I felt afraid for him.

Mum raised her eyebrows. 'It's crucial to try AA. Maybe they'll help.'

Dad's eyes bulged. 'Me? Alcoholic? Come off it, Genn. Alcoholics are dirty, unshaven blokes. They swill metho and sleep in pig pens at the saleyards.' Why, he worked harder than three men. Could lift a tree trunk strainer post unaided – and often did. Alcoholic? Not a respectable fellow like him with home and family to support. 'Genn, I must have something to see me through this.'

Mum's eyes blazed. 'Don't you think it's time to stop?'

Dad hoarse. 'Please. I need enough to dry me out. Drive me to the pub.'

Mum's bitter laugh. 'Certainly not.'

I hated seeing this proud and confident man pleading.

'A drink will have me back to normal.'

Mum gave a great sigh. 'That's what you always say.'

'My life depends on it, Genn.'

Finally, with a great sigh, she acquiesced. He slumped into the cabin beside her. She drove him the twenty-odd miles to the nearest village.

By morning, the one small bottle of brandy she had allowed him was gone. Dad looked worse – if that were possible. Face ashen, uncontrollable tremor. He stumbled around seeking his holy grail – a missed bottle.

Mum clucked like an angry hen. 'I knew buying that brandy was a mistake. Now you're paying for your foolishness.'

Dad stood before her, grasping the kitchen table for support. Shrinking before my eyes. This was the worst spree ever. I sensed that our father teetered on the brink of some abyss.

It felt hard enough dealing with my own fears. Little remained among my coping mechanisms to offer Druce the emotional support he needed. A little boy lost, he hovered in the background. At an age when every lad needs a strong male role model, his face mirrored despair and bewilderment.

The mail contractor brought bread and other supplies. Including illicit booze. Dad struggled up to the mailbox, having a lengthy natter to the driver.

Mum glowered through the window. 'What's he up to?

Dad tottered back to the house. He made a great show of putting two bottles of wine on the table. 'Just to tide me over. Then I'll be OK.'

'How long am I expected to tolerate a man in your condition – if you call yourself a man?'

'I need enough to dry me out.' His strangled voice haunts me still. 'You pour for me – just as much as you think.'

With an air of suppressed fury, she poured a very small amount. 'That's all you're getting.'

'Please, Genn. A little more.'

Mum corked the bottle with a finality that made the stopper squeak.

Dad downed the half-glass at one gulp. A forced smile. 'I'll go and have a snooze in the sun. Fresh air will do me good.' He picked up a rug, lurching down the paddock.

Mum groaned. 'Bet that bloody mailman's hidden more grog.'

Anxiety roiled in my gut. Would this terrible bender ever end?

Time dragged.

In the golden glow of late afternoon, Mum voiced our collective unease. 'Where's your father? He should be back.'

Vance looked thoughtful. 'The mail truck stopped near that small culvert across the creek. I'll take a look.' He found six bottles of wine, two empty. 'No sign of Dad.'

'Where can he be?' Her face was a study in anxiety. She told Druce. 'You wait in the house. Give us a coo-ee if he returns.'

My little brother looked terrified. I guess he hated being left alone.

She snapped. 'Do as you're told.'

We left his forlorn figure on the veranda.

I squelched over marshy ground. A scream of plovers whooshed away at my approach. Scrambled through tea trees. My legs and arms scratched and bleeding.

'Dad! Daddy! Are you there?' My heart lurched, then raced.

Was that a body, half-hidden in the undergrowth?

Sagging at the knees, I edged closer. Exhaled a great, ragged breath. Failing light, a twisted stump. Transformed into the human form.

Mist blotted the tops of eucalypts. Crept along the brow of the hill, and into our valley. Stole the golden light.

Damp and chilled, I shouted, 'Daddy! Where are you?' I guessed that in his frail state, he would be unlikely to survive the night.

We scoured the home paddock. Running out of places to search. Not a sign of him since that last glimpse of his back.

Twilight drank the last colour from the day. Starling twittered, ready for sleep.

Mum had aged ten years. 'Any sign?'

Vance shook his head. 'I'll scour the top paddock. Mum, you and Vivi look in this area. Dessie, scout along the road.'

We avoided each other's eyes. I trembled with fear and exhaustion.

A catch in Mum's voice, 'But – how could he get so far – in his state?'

The biting wind might know the answer.

My teeth chittered. I drew my old cardigan around thin shoulders. Forced weary legs along the rutted road. I followed no religion, but scraped up a prayer. Someone out there might hear my plea for guidance. A voice in the wilderness cried, 'Dad! Where are you, Daddy?'

A chorus of croaking frogs mocked my cries. Nauseated at the thought of calling neighbours into the search.

Vance signalled to us in the fading light. I stumbled to his side. Shocked to see Dad, grey and unmoving, slumped on the damp rug.

Mum spoke for all of us. 'My God – is he dead?'

Vance gave a tight smile. 'Dead drunk.' He had found Dad collapsed. 'Still clutching an empty bottle of whisky.'

We half-carried, half-dragged him home. Druce met us at the door, pale and tremulous.

Mum snapped, 'Dad's all right.'

He blinked back tears – and so did I. My hug. 'He's going to be all right.' Hoping I was telling the truth.

Dad raved most of the night. Shouting at invisible demons. Nobody slept. I dreaded another morning.

The grey light of dawn found him beset by unseen monsters. He screamed and yelled, sweating profusely.

Mum did her best to feed him spoonfuls of chicken broth, face creased with anxiety. 'You must have something.'

He managed a little, with difficulty.

Never before had we felt so helpless. Or seen Daddy so ill. Small comfort to know he had always recovered. It didn't occur to us that he might need urgent medical attention. Later, in my nursing studies, I learnt about delusional melancholia – delirium tremens. Chilled to read it frequently leads to death.

Dad stumbled in and out of bed. 'Want to go outside.' Within seconds, he staggered back. terror in his eyes. 'Down near that lagoon of wine, there's a mermaid. A most gorgeous creature. Dressed in clothes of many hues.' He pointed with a tremulous finger. 'She wanted me to go down there in the nude. But I couldn't do that.'

'Lie down, Dad. Please rest.'

'Rest? Don't you see she's trying get me? Wants to outdo your mother.' He put a quivering hand on my shoulder. 'Please! Go into the bedroom first. See if anyone's there. Shut the windows so she can't take me.' He crawled under the top sheet, shaking. Pulled it over his head. 'Stay here. Please.'

By the following day, his mermaid had vanished. Dare we hope the crisis had passed? He only managed broth or fluids for a week.

A fortnight passed. His pallor faded. Slowly, slowly, the spring returned to his step. It felt lovely to have our intelligent, funny Dad back. But even after this brush with death, his addiction had the upper hand. It took only a single drink…

We waved Dad away to visit his sister, our Aunt Aileen, at Newcastle. Later, the family heard a news broadcast: 'Unknown man with red hair rescued from his vehicle after crashing. A Bedford truck left the road at Minmi, coming to rest in a grove of small saplings. The trees undoubtedly saved the driver's life. He has amnesia, so is unable to help police with their inquiries.'

Vivi laughed. 'Red hair, Bedford truck. Wouldn't it be funny if that were Dad?'

Mum's eyes bulged. 'Don't be so damned silly.'

Aileen rang a short while later, 'There's been accident near Minmi.'

Mum paled. 'Accident?'

'They've just identified Joly. Admitted to Newcastle hospital.'

Mum paled. 'My God. Is he all right?'

'He's fine. Suffered some sort of blackout. Or fell asleep at the wheel.'

'Huh! Suppose he'd been drinking.'

A long silence. 'No, no. I don't believe he'd touched a drop.'

Aileen called again next day. 'Joly has some residual amnesia. Don't mind telling you, it's scared him. He's promised to attend AA.'

Mum slammed down the receiver. 'Trust that woman to make your father see sense. God knows, I've tried often enough.'

Traffic accidents are rarely positive events. But I doubt whether Dad would have sought help had it not been for his. A single meeting at AA was enough. Dad clawed his way back from the abyss to sobriety. It was marvellous to have a father who could go to town without worrying whether he'd return in one piece.

About then, Dad brought home a couple of antique bottles.

Mum said, 'Get rid of them.'

Someone informed her they were valuable. Long after Dad had lost interest, Mum dragged him off to distant sites to dig up rare specimens. She amassed a large collection. Made swaps and good buys, won silver cups and colourful ribbons. Some might say, a strange hobby for the wife of a recovering alcoholic.

Conquer the Sugarloaf

The Sugarloaf crouched in harsh morning light. A volcanic peak, it dwarfed surrounding hills. Dare we venture onto its steep flanks?

I glanced at Vivi. 'What do you reckon?'

'Let's go.' Vivi bubbled her excitement.

The huge beast towered above us, daunting close up. Our first eager steps left the foothills far behind. The incline grew steeper. Gasping for every breath, we clutched tussocks, shrubs or logs. Anything to haul ourselves higher. I welcomed the soothing caress of a breeze.

My initial burst of enthusiasm gave way to grim determination. I mustn't let it beat me. The sun climbed too, a solace at first. Almost at its zenith, hot rays seared bare skin.

Less than halfway to our goal, my doubts began. Doubled. Multiplied. I struggled from shade to shade, shirt damp with sweat, brow dripping. Every muscle in my arms and legs ached. Why put myself through this?

Vivi took the lead. Glancing back with a cheeky grin. 'What's keeping you?'

Energy levels surged. I could never let my kid sister reach the summit first.

A gaggle of black hitchhikers swarmed along for the ride. Clung to the back of my damp shirt. Resisting attempts to brush them away. 'Feel like the old man of the sea,' I groaned. 'Only I've a whole bunch of critters to carry around.'

She sighed. 'This contingent of bush flies shows no mercy.'

Two switches with leaves finally did the trick.

The sun blazed in hot, still air. I sat under a kurrajong. Admired its bell-shaped blossoms.

'The name derives from the Dharuk language, garrajun. I believe it means fishing line – they used to make it from the kurragong bark.'

'Really?' Vivi stroked the bark. 'The miracle of items discovered in Nature's warehouse.'

'Indigenous people not only survived, but thrived in the bush. They used all sorts of found objects.'

'Rendered stuff safe to eat, diluting toxins in streams.'

We opened backpacks.

'Don't know about you,' I said. 'But I'm ravenous.'

'Me too. It's well past lunchtime.'

We munched corned beef sandwiches. Devoured apples. Gulped tea, and shared a last banana.

I laughed. 'Nothing like fresh air and exercise for the appetite. My hunger's only half-satisfied.'

She nodded. 'It might be a long afternoon.'

Cool shadows tempted me to linger. Or take a leisurely walk home.

Vivi said, 'We'd be fools not to complete the walk.'

I laughed. 'How dare you read my thoughts? Let's get it over with.'

The mountain had become a parable for life itself. Challenging, difficult. Often not much fun. Just there, to be tackled and overcome. A bit like grasping for freedom. Or finding a fulfilling career.

The summit tantalised. Almost there, yet forever out of reach. Elusive as a dream.

Our sneakers sent light shale pinging away with a metallic ring. Stunted trees with large, shiny leaves struggled for existence in the stony environment. We pushed aside dogwood bushes. The stink lingered on our hands.

Fought on. And on. Knife-edged grass and prickly pear slashed at our trousers.

Lungs gasped for mercy.

Would our excursion ever end?

It happened so suddenly, we both gasped. A plateau unfolded before our delighted gaze.

Vivi eyes gleamed. A cairn of stones, and a black direction indicator. 'We've done it, sis.'

'Aha! The triangulation, or trig station. Wonder when the government started putting these survey marks on high hills and mountains? A boon for hikers like us.'

Her brow creased. 'But what do they survey?

'Daddy says land boundaries. Roads and bridges, all that stuff.'

'Let's celebrate.'

'Oh, look!'

We giggled in delight. A willy-wagtail danced our very own sarabande of victory. The bird took flight.

Vivi grinned, 'Now, sis, it's our turn.'

Linking arms, we danced, laughed and shouted at the top of our lungs,

A panorama of hills stretched in every direction. Omniscient, all powerful, we could vanquish the world. Roads wended, rivers twisted. Patchworks of fields, shrunken farmhouses.

Our friend Ross had fought in the Second World War. He'd told me about peaks in Italy. 'Most had a castle perched on top.'

I laughed. 'When I'm old and very rich, I'll build a castle here.'

'One castle?' Vivi raised her eyebrows. 'Make it two – you live in one, I'll have the other.'

We chuckled with the sheer exuberance of being young.

Hills changed robes. Switched from violet to purple and indigo.

Shadows lengthened. Time for home. Throbbing muscles meant I'd pay the price tomorrow. But who cared?

Some day far away, I'd share tales of my adventures with grandchildren. Just as Granny's yarns of her bush rambles and romance had brought a sparkle to our eyes.

Breaking Barriers

Cousin Ethan thought of Julia as his soulmate. They had exchanged emails after he was widowed. Ruby had suffered for years. Her passing came as a blessed relief. Ethan, of course, felt lost. Julia relished the prospect of meeting him again. He sounded eager to show her friend, Xanthe, and herself around.

'I'm all yours on Thursday. Just tell me what you'd like to do.'

All mine? There's always been a frisson between them. He'd visited briefly last summer, the first time in a decade. Tall, silver hair, captivating smile. Sexy, despite the moustache. The first ten minutes, Ethan was by himself.

He grinned. 'Ruby's outside, having a smoke.'

She found it odd that his wife hadn't come inside to say hello. Could she be that desperate for a fag? Only later did I discover she was at my place under protest.

When Ruby limped in, her smile sagged into shock. Puffy face, the colour of liver. Gasping for breath. Ten years ago, she had been young, vibrant.

At afternoon tea, Julia and Ethan laughed over family stories. Old tales waltzed with new. Ruby had little to say. Doone had hoped to enjoy a long, relaxed evening, over dinner and a few glasses of Sauvignon blanc.

But Ethan explained. 'Ruby must rush off to catch up with an old friend.' He seemed reluctant to leave, holding Doone's hand seconds longer than necessary. Ruby was already in the car.

Later that year, Ethan rang Doone, voice choked with emotion. Ruby's death was expected. Yet it was a shock, as these things are. Previous commitments meant she gave the funeral a miss. Sent a magnificent bouquet of flowers. He confided that the last months had been hell, for both of them, given Ruby's multiple surgeries. Doone had had no idea. She sensed the poor man was torn between grief, and relief, at having the nightmare finally over.

Emails flew to and fro. At her age, the love part of life seemed over. But why was she smiling for no reason? In her youth she wouldn't have dreamt of a liaison with a close blood relation. But whose business would it be if they... An elderly couple... Of course, eyebrows might be raised. Doone could imagine gossips whispering, have you heard?

Still, she wasn't about to shout such news from Centrepoint Tower.

Early one morning, Xanthe and Doone arrived in Melbourne. Settled into their youth hostel. A misnomer, since many of the guests were elderly. They loved the elegance and charm of Little Collins Street. The boutiques tucked away in arcades. The aroma of coffee shops. Giggling their way through Wednesday, exchanging confidences. Xanthe was on the lookout for linen trousers. Doone bought a silver bracelet with a heart, and snapped up a layered chiffon scarf in greys, with hints of mauve.

They decided Melbourne was the shoe capital of Australia. Never had either of them seen so many different designs. All teetered on heels higher than Mount Blanc; they glittered in appropriately placed lighting.

Red Japanese lanterns glowed a welcome to a tea house. The 'girls' sipped a variety of blends. Bowing hostesses in scarlet kimonos urged them to buy. They drooled over a strawberry, blueberry and raspberry flan, steeped in curaçao, with a port wine jelly topping.

Xanthe grinned. 'Wicked.'

In the bar of Young and Jackson in Swanston Street, they admired a certain young lady. Her charms had graced magazine covers. Inspired poems. Wines had been named for her – the famous nude painting, *Chloe*, by Joseph Lefebvre, 1875. Over a gin and tonic, Doone learnt that she was a National Trust treasure.

She lit a candle for Ruby in the cathedral. Surely in a better place, God rest her soul. It's barely three months since she passed. Surprised to hear that Ethan had found someone on the net.

A perfect match, he'd said in his email. 'We've known each other in a previous life. Julia's manager of a shoe shop. Plans to move into my place soon.'

Xanthe looked up from the laptop screen. She laughed. 'Ethan's not one to let the grass grow.'

Doone bit her lip. Knowing how Ethan must feel. His house like a prison, acid with the taste of grief and loss. Missing the companionship. The cherishing, and skin-to-skin contact. Desperate to affirm he's still alive. At seventy, there wasn't a lot of time for him to lose.

After Ted died, Doone recalled being horrified at the thought of going solo for the next thirty years. Knowing a woman over fifty has little hope of finding that special someone. About as likely as picking up a gold nugget in George Street, she thought. Anyway, that's Pooh sticks under the bridge. Oh, why hadn't she gone to Ruby's funeral?

Tonight she was to meet Ethan again. A new hairdo. Nails polished. Chanel No 5. Carla Zampatti chiffon blouse…

Xanthe chuckled. 'Doone, you're all glitter and glamour. Shame Ethan's found Julia.'

Doone shrugged. 'Good for him.' But why did her voice sound so unconvinced?

Xanthe waved, off with a pal. 'See you in the morning.'

Doone's tram rattled along to Northcote. Ethan had arranged to meet her at the theatre. She looked forward to a new play by Lucille de Vos, *Wicked Liaisons*. And tomorrow she'd be meeting the lovely Julia…

Ethan's gags made her laugh. Over a gin and tonic, he kept glancing Doone's way. She felt amazed at the admiration in his eyes.

'You don't look anything like seventy – more fifty.'

Her cheeks burnt. Who was it that said humans are the only animals who blush – and the only ones that need to?

She pictured Julia adjusting a purple shoe until it sat just so, a jewel in her hands.

The play was full of laughter and intrigue. Just the tonic Doone needed…

Ethan drove Doone back to the hostel, his phone set for early. His lips flamed against hers. She watched him leave for the long drive home.

Friday yawned into one of those glittering days of late summer. The air breathed all around them with the promise of a lovely autumn.

Ethan arrived, with an apology. 'Julia couldn't join us. Staff problems.'

'Shame.' she lied. A silent prayer of thanks. 'Uhh, none of my business, of course, but take it slowly. Don't make any moves you might regret.'

Moves? My goodness, she'd move into his arms right now. A shiver at the memory of his lips on hers. Longing for those strong hands caressing her. She took the front seat beside him.

Xanthe chatted brightly from the back. 'Doone's right. Once someone moves in…'

His car nosed out into the traffic. 'I'll show you the mansions of St Kilda.'

Leafy blocks. Half-hidden architectural treasures. They made suitable expressions of admiration. Headed into the suburbs. Explored the Dandenongs. William Rickett's sculpture and contemplation garden.

'You've always been my favourite cousin.'

Her heart missed a beat. Julia. His shoe shop manager girlfriend.

Scarlet shoes, tucked sides, heels taller than the Eiffel Tower.

Cousin? Damn, damn and double damn. Oh, why was she so attracted to him?

He grinned. 'Julia's a lovely lady.'

Xanthe's voice was bright with fake delight. 'We can't wait to meet her.'

Green satin slingbacks, matching flounce at front. Heels like Mount Everest.

If only they'd shared this date before...

A Cubist exhibition. The sign said, 'I paint things as I think them, not as I see them.'

Ethan so close he almost touched. Chemistry zinged between them.

Xanthe peered through her specs. 'Can you believe it? The cubists started in the antipodes, thirty years before Europe.'

Doone shook her head. Only half-listening. Eyed cubes. Squares. Triangles... They gazed at an installation. *Fractals of swirling colour. She floated away on red, blue, and purple... Ropes of light twisted and unfurled. Twisted again. A DNA double helix. Shoes walked by, brown. A man's trouser leg. The hint of a skirt. Hands and hearts transformed into swirling eddies of colour. An underwater world. Ripples morphed into giant waves.*

Everything and nothing was what it seemed. A painting – or was it? Glass. Bottle. Plate. Edges overlapped. Merged. The bottle showed the opposite side, hid the label...

Birdsong... Barking dog... The rattle of an approaching train...

Doone had thought herself calm. In control. Love was for the young. An inner voice urged, crack the barriers. Move against convention.

They admired Seurat, Degas. Elements of living were analysed. Taken apart. An assemblage of thoughts and emotions. Duchamp's *Nude* walked downstairs. One. Or two. Or three.

Somehow, Doone found herself in the café. They relaxed in the aroma of freshly brewed coffee. Settled for slices of flavoursome apple pie, loaded with whipped cream.

Next to her, he leant closer. 'What's that perfume?'

'Chanel No. 5. Worn it since I was nineteen. Daddy once gave me ten pounds as a present – never dreamt I'd splurge it on a perfume.'

Xanthe chuckled. 'Good for you.'

His hand brushed hers. 'Such a lovely, fruity aroma.'

Doone gulped mouthfuls of scalding tea. Barely noticing.

Ethan picked up the bill.

Shocking pink suede shoe with diamanté toes. Winged stiletto heel.

Xanthe left with friends for the evening.

Back in town, Ethan and Doone dined in the Sherlock Holmes pub, a cellar location. Barramundi, fragrant with lemon.

She bit into a crisp salad of mixed lettuce, red capsicum and flavoursome potatoes. 'Almost as good as home-grown ones.'

Ethan grinned. 'You're right.'

The Sauvignon blanc was excellent.

'To us.'

Glasses clinked.

Ethan looked thoughtful. 'We've met just six times in our whole lives.' He reeled off the dates.

She felt amazed that he remembered.

He told of his many visits to Sydney on business, along with his late wife. 'I longed to visit you. Guess Ruby was jealous. So…'

Thanks, Ruby, she mused. Fancy her thinking me a threat. I was married to Ted. Ah, the exquisite pleasure of multiple orgasms and lusts of the spirit. 'It makes me sad to think you never had the chance to meet my husband.'

'I regret that, too. We might have become friends.'

They lingered over dinner. Explored spiritual connections. First sexual encounters. The pain of unrequited love.

A brief romance with Arthur, her first love, slipped out. 'He'll always hold a corner of my heart. Second cousin, twice removed.' It was warm but she shivered. What's this thing I have about cousins? 'I've never told anyone that before.'

Ethan grinned. 'Let's drink to that.' He glanced at his watch. 'It's getting late. I'd better sober up before that forty K drive home. Feel like a walk across the Yarra?'

'Sounds good.' Didn't he know she'd cross rings of fire just to be with him? Warning herself, Doone, take a grip.

Wilner shoes, cerise pink and glitter. Peep-toes and heels that reach the sky.

They explored the shadowy casino. Smelt the greed. Heard the chatter of poker chips. Sad faces. Set faces. Calculating eyes. A cascade gurgled over rocks. Sculptural figures soared. A young girl in red pirouetted and danced.

Ethan sighed. 'My parking meter expires in five minutes.'

It had been four hours since they arrived back in town. She gulped. Why had fate dealt her this cousin-card again? Doone recalled her one date with Arthur, after months of anticipation. Him with a fiancée waiting interstate. A brief day. Same sense of pleasure edged with loss. She forced a laugh. 'Where did that time go?'

They lingered on the bridge. Casino lights glittered, mirrored by the Yarra. Flares exploded out front. One. Two. Three. Four… Thery stood, side by side. Lost in shifting time zones. Engulfed by the heat.

A blaze of red and black patent leather, in contrast with the lustre of lizard skin, shiny patent heel, straight from Venus.

Crushing hug, lingering kiss. He looked back but kept walking…

Ethan telephoned not long after she returned to Sydney, upset. 'Julia's been two-timing me…'

He arrives tomorrow.

Purple silk sheets. A sprinkle of rose petals. Haunting melody, something from Scheherazade, *perhaps? Nuances of elephants, lions, tigers. Dappled light. Perfumed pink candles. She'd stroke her body with fragrant unguents and creams. Smooth rouge around her nipples. Kohl for her eyes…*

Girl Without a Face

Not a cap stirred on that grey Saturday morning. Lonely, deserted corridors. Who'd believe that eight hundred girls lived in Queen Mary Probationer Nurses' Home? The musty, antiseptic smell made me crave the perfume of soap and powder at home.

A number of nurses had gone missing in action. I ached for my friend Clara. And, months earlier, Jane had disappeared too. Along with her dreams of becoming matron. Our Jane with her super confidence, worn down by the vitriol dished out under the guise of discipline. And I happened upon one nurse, clutching a bundle of clothing, bed lamp and radio.

'Leaving?' I said.

Guilt suffused her face. 'No, no, no. Just…home for days off.'

I never saw her again.

I gazed way below my window. Imaginary friends, Louise and Archibald, pottered in their tiny garden. The weeping peach tree was ablaze with pink this spring. The old couple seemed a picture of animation and good cheer. Was their capacity for optimism the secret of a long and happy life? How could I seize the moment this grey Saturday? Perhaps join the surreal world of some movie, suck Jaffas and pretend to be a carefree child.

The jangle of my buzzer. I gave a start. Surely I hadn't misread the roster? I ran to answer the phone. Fearing a blast from Sister Flapper.

'Is that you, Dessie? Guess who?'

That lilting drawl. I'd know it anywhere. Dessie, my pet name… The years I'd imagined Rick calling. The clever things I'd say… But now, lost for words, I pretended not to recognise his voice. Playing for time.

Disappointment in his voice. 'Rick... Richard Knight.'

My hand hurt from clutching the receiver. 'What a surprise.'

'Your father gave me your address. And as I was in Sydney...'

A courtesy call. Silly me, thinking it might be something more. But why would Daddy suggest Rick get in touch? He'd done everything to keep us apart. Was he hoping to lure me home?

I kept my voice non-committal. 'Thanks for calling. It's lovely to hear a voice from home.'

There was an edge of desperation to Rick's voice. 'And...I was wondering. Could we go out?'

I could scarcely believe my ears. Asking me for a date – at last. Best not to appear over-eager. 'That sounds fun.'

Rick would arrive within half an hour.

I pirouetted along the corridor.

A third-year nurse regarded me with disdain. 'Won the lottery?'

Dizzy with elation, I looked her straight in the eye. 'Better than that...my boyfriend has arrived.'

The words had such a positive ring. I laughed out loud. Two years since we'd last danced. I'd long given up hopes... All my dreams come true, aglow right there in that austere room.

A quick comb-up of my brown hair. Smoothed on make-up. Pink lipstick. Was that radiant face really mine? My second chance.

I agonised over what to wear. Slipping into a cream blouse, the Peter Pan collar edged with lace. A brown woollen skirt and olive-green jumper.

Rick was taller than my memory of him. Surprised to find him pacing the visitor's room. A shy boy, rather than the man of the world my parents had feared.

In that moment of hesitation, we stared at each other. His firm hand closed on mine. The look in his eyes brought that old tingle.

'Dessie... it's great to see you.'

The caress of his voice. I caught my breath. He looked cute in black slacks and a beautiful hand-knitted yellow jumper. The sort every girl of the era crafted for their man...

Rick gave an embarrassed cough, freed my hand. 'I thought we'd catch a movie.'

'Excellent.'

We took a taxi. Rick walked on the street side as gentlemen did in olden days, with splashes of mud a problem. The caress of his eyes met mine. The meeting was surreal, a curious blend of bitter-sweet memories and first date. I dare not ask if he were still engaged. It would be the worst folly to confirm a rival with a winner's trophy, third finger left hand. And why didn't Rick ask about my life as a nurse?

I feared we must squeeze this whole relationship into a few hours.

At lunch, Rick chose a garish café. Fluorescent lighting. Plastic-topped tables. Like one of the cheap places in some country town. I thought, don't be a snob. But my nose wrinkled at the odour of french fries and old oil.

We lingered over cappuccinos.

Rick pulled some tickets out of his pocket. 'Have I got a treat in store for you. We're off to the grand final.' A lopsided grin. 'Bought these at the last minute.'

I didn't want to spoil his excitement. But knew nothing of the sport.

We took our places. The shiver of his hand, squeezing mine. St George played Manly. The crowd revved with excitement. Waved banners of red and maroon. Blew whistles. A little terrier trotted around in team colours.

Everything was draped with balloons and streamers. Rick explained points of the play. I only half-listened, intoxicated by that fairy tale called love. An abstract impression of running figures in red, white and maroon. Ritualistic scrums. Tries from St George. Roars of approval.

A decisive victory of twenty to zero for St George. Rick shouted his excitement. Supporters roared. Car horns blared. A huge hug. My heart lurched. I thought he was going to kiss me. Aching with disappointment.

Rick brushed back his thatch of blond hair. 'How about a five o'clock movie?'

I collected a late pass at Queen Mary. A taxi sped us to one of the city cinemas. I could never recall, then or now, which show we saw. Not a word or single image remained. The dream of seeing him again had eluded me for so long. Intoxicated by that boy at my side.

A chicken dinner. Darkness cast its spell over the city. Barely two hours of our date remained. I didn't want to miss a moment of his company.

Rick was booked into a hotel in the lower end of town. 'It's called the People's Palace.'

Shabby clientele with broad-brimmed hats congregated in reception. My heart sank at the pretentious title. A haven for country people of limited means, I thought.

Rick said, 'Coming upstairs to…uh…freshen up?'

Nice girls didn't go to a boy's room. Not in 1959. But I didn't plan to miss a single moment of this interlude, the sweetest day of my life.

The spotty desk clerk handed Rick the key. Leered at me. Jumping to conclusions…

A lift, acrid with old oil, creaked toward the third floor. Rick led the way along a gloomy corridor. Fumbled to open the door.

My double take: a double bed. I could imagine my friend, Fleur: 'Oh come on, Seberg… What did you expect?'

Rick glimpsed my expression. He said quickly, 'It…it was the only one they had.'

I perched on the edge of a sagging mattress. A naked bulb. Yellowing wallpaper. Gimcrack furniture. Determined to soar above such things.

Rick peered into the foxed mirror. Made a pretense of combing his hair. At last, he sat beside me, trembling. Anguish in his voice. 'Oh, Dessie.. Dessie… How I longed to take you out…but you lived so far away. And, to tell the truth, I was afraid of your dad.'

To think that my father's reputation as a boxer…

'So that's why you never…' My hollow laugh.

Embarrassed, he said, 'I know it's silly…but I was younger then. When your dad said you were in Sydney, I had to come.'

We melted into each other's arms. Never had kisses tasted sweeter.

He caressed my shoulders. 'I've not forgotten you since that first night we met.'

'I've always liked you too.' My feelings went much deeper. I thrilled to the forbidden touch of my breasts.

Hoarsely, he whispered. 'Dessie… Oh, Dessie.'

How I longed to float away with the running tide. But Nice Girls didn't. Not in 1959. Not with the shadowy figure of an unknown fiancée in the background. A girl without a face.

I cursed myself for lack of courage. Afraid of getting pregnant. Afraid of becoming the butt of ribald humour in some anonymous bar. But a few brief moments of passion would never satisfy my need to be cherished.

Gently, I removed his caressing hands. 'No, Rick.'

'It's no different from touching your skin at the beach.'

We both knew differently.

My throat ached. Tears unshed. Never had I needed inner strength more. 'It's been a wonderful day, Rick. Truly wonderful. But I must go.'

One last, tantalising glimpse of him through the cab window. I waved until he disappeared.

I woke on a high. Trembled at the memory of his taut body. Shivered at a certain smile, the caress of his voice. By afternoon, my sunny mood had twisted into knots of uncertainty. I left for work under weeping skies, hands thrust deep into my uniform pockets.

Rick's 'Don't know when I'll see you again' carried the sour taste of goodbye.

A 'Thought for the Day' leapt from Sister's desk calendar. 'And on the morrow, all is over. A dream is over. The memory of it brings a sad sensation as if someone had died.'

Every summer for years he visited my parents' farm. I like to think he asked after me…

The Burning Sixpence

Gloria shuddered to a stop, in an intersection. The glint of huge eyes met hers. Clatter of hooves. A giant black horse galloped her way. Maniacal laughter echoed down the years. A scream howled into the darkness. Her Mozart concert program crumpled in her sweating hand.

Plump and middle-aged to the casual observer. Deep within, a vulnerable little girl. Floral dress. Peter Pan collar. Short legs of childhood.

About to be trampled underfoot.

A warning shout. 'Look out!'

Gloria couldn't budge. A bystander dragged her to safety. Headlights engulfed them both. A huge vehicle roared over the spot where she had just been.

She babbled. 'The horse… It almost crushed me.'

He blinked. 'You're in shock, love. There weren't no horse. Just a blooming great truck. Could've killed us both.'

Another flashback, Gloria thought. Would they ever leave her in peace?' Uh, thanks. I…uh…need a cab.'

Her saviour flagged one down. 'Go home and have a good rest now, love. You need it.'

Teeth chattering, she slumped onto the back seat.

'Where to, ma'am?'

Her thoughts flittered. Moths dazzled by a lamp. Refusing to settle.

The taxi driver glared at her in the rear-view mirror. 'Am I to sit here all night?'

Gloria stammered the address.

The cabbie kept demanding directions.

'What's wrong with you?' Gloria snapped. 'You're effing well doing the driving.' Shocked by her own failure to observe middle-class values.

He slammed on the brakes. 'That's it, lady. Get out and walk.'

Gloria watched the red tail lights disappear. Home was only blocks away. But what sort of driver abandoned a woman in the middle of the night?

Gravel crunched underfoot. A burly fellow approached. 'See you home, darling?'

Gloria's feet gained wings. She hadn't run so fast in years.

'Don't be like that, sweetheart.'

She sped past two vacant allotments. Reached her row of terraces. Gasping for breath, she stepped inside. Slid three deadlocks into place. Rushed to the bathroom. Heaved. Flushed. And rinsed the acid taste of vomit from her mouth.

A sombre face stared back from the mirrored wall. Pallid skin, auburn hair.

That morning, like almost every other Friday of her adult life, Gloria had visited her hairdresser. The new girl needed coaching to tease her locks into the exaggerated bouffant style Gloria preferred. The height of fashion in her youth.

Gloria simpered. 'Don't forget my Bill Haley kiss curl.'

Coco, the twenty-something lass, looked puzzled. 'Bill Haley?'

'Way before your time, dear. A rock singer, from the fifties. Use lots of hairspray.' She covered her nose and mouth, enveloped in a hissing cloud of lacquer.

Coco exchanged a glance of disdain with Madame, her boss, who hated to see a client leave her salon looking so – twee. 'Don't tell people where you had it done, will you?'

'You are awful,' Gloria had giggled. 'I wouldn't be me without my hair and nails.' She displayed her long red talons.

Mother had said that Mr Right would find her. But youth sped into middle age. Unmarried in her sixties, Gloria felt betrayed. She gave up the office job to care for ageing parents, moved back home. They said it was a daughter's duty. Funny, they didn't expect the same from Vance.

Her brother never did a hand's turn for them. The perfect son. She shopped and cooked and scrubbed. Endured a slew of maternal criticism. Angry. Frustrated. A word of appreciation would have made all the difference.

Father died in a traffic accident. Mother lingered, semi-comatose. Gloria kept a vigil at the bedside, craving words of affection. Shortly before she died, mother rallied. Gave Vance a long glance of adoration. Breathed one last, tiny breath.

Gloria had a sudden fear that she had never existed.

So here I am, she thought. Still struggling to make sense of life. But after Mother died, Gloria took her courage in both hands. Bought her terrace and made her first visit to the local. She enjoyed evenings of laughter and noisy conversation. Even liked the aroma of ale, though a glass of alcohol had never passed her lips.

New friends giggled over her lime and bitter. 'What sort of drink is that?' They chuckled at this quaint relic from the past, bouffant hairstyle, and heavy hand with the rouge, all part of the package. Called her a character. Gloria laughed along with them. Should anyone think about it at all, they mistook her mirth for happiness.

By then, the auburn hair of her youth needed a touch of the dye brush. She giggled. Mother would be scandalised. Only hussies tinted their locks or went to bars. She would have approved the concerts, but.

Ashamed to find herself on the brink of tears on several occasions, Gloria sought help. Not sure if she were doing the right thing. Desperate enough not to care.

Jenny, friend of a friend, understood these things. Warm smile, gentle voice. She indicated a settee, with bright cushions. Produced a box of tissues as if it were the most natural thing in the world. 'Tell me about it.'

Gloria wiped her eyes. 'I pretend to be having fun. Who has patience with a sad friend?'

'So you're the life of the party?'

Gloria bit her lip. 'Sort of.' She thought of occasions the group had laughed at her. All the hurt and tears poured out.

Jenny understood. The first person in her adult life to do so. Probably ever. Gloria exchanged one sodden tissue for another. She told of the challenging relationship with her mother. And of her brother's terrifying pranks.

Jenny shook her head. 'Have you discussed it with him?'

Gloria swallowed. 'Never.'

On Jenny's urging, she tackled Big Brother about it. Expecting a 'sorry'.

She said, 'Vance declared it had never happened.'

'Siblings often have different recollections of their childhood.' Jenny suggested she treat her life as a book. 'Meditate away the painful episodes.'

Gloria slipped into her embroidered silk nightdress. Lights out. Eyes closed. Hour after hour, she loaded the charred pages of her life onto barges. One would leave and another take it's place. Barge after barge carried away anger, hurt and misunderstandings. Exhausted, she groped around for a glass of water. Waited for her sleeping pill to take effect.

Drifting in that crepuscule zone between sleep and waking, she saw Mother again. The first time since she'd died. The scent of mimosa and vanilla made her yearn to run into her arms. Seek approval one more time.

'Mother.' Her voice echoed into the hollow distance of time. But the image had vanished. Gloria found herself lost in a forest of gigantic people. Arms had morphed into limbs and leaves.

A voice mocked. 'Wicked, that's what you are. Always have been, always will be.'

Nightmares galloped into her room. The maniac in control of that black horse jeered and laughed. Hooves drummed on the hard earth. She couldn't move, let alone run, no more than seven or eight at the time. Again and again, Big Brother drove the snorting animal towards her. The mare all flaring nostrils and wild eyes.

Like a rodeo rider harries a frightened calf, Big Brother made another attack. Wheeled the horse. And another. Stopping just in time. His crazed laughter echoed down the corridors of time.

She stood mute. Frozen to the spot.

At last, Big Brother brought the panting horse to a stop. Leapt to the ground. Shoved a coin into her hand. 'Here's sixpence. Keep yer mouth shut, OK?'

Mother trotted up on the chestnut mare. Smart in jodhpurs and riding boots. Gloria trembled. Wary, as ever, when that stern parent appeared.

Big Brother smirked at Gloria. Behind Mother's back, he put a finger on his lips for silence. 'Shall I take off the saddle for you, Mother?'

Mum beamed. 'My, what a good boy you are.' She noticed Gloria's tear-streaked face. 'What's this about?'

The child hung her head.

'Can you throw any light on this, Vance?'

Big Brother shrugged.

'Dogs and children must be shown who is the boss.' Mother scowled. 'What have I done to deserve a child like you? Speak up, miss.'

Gloria opened her tightly clenched hand. She meant to show Mother the price of silence. But the sixpence had vanished. Burnt its way inside her hand.

'It's wicked not to answer.' Mother stalked away.

Gloria washed and washed her hand. Determined to find the burning sixpence. Lost because I'm wicked.

Mother strode into the room. 'Don't forget your face. Oh, let me do it.' She roughly scrubbed the tender skin with a soapy rag. It smelt musty. 'As if I haven't enough to do.'

'Ouch. It stings my eyes.'

'Next time, my girl, do it yourself.'

All so long ago, Gloria thought. How can these things still have the power to wound me?

The golden veil of evening. Gloria checked the TV guide. A series of B-grade movies didn't appeal. She flicked off the switch.

Next moment, the picture leapt right back – and in brilliant colour. She gaped. The old set showed only black and white. But she glimpsed a girl in a red bikini. Can't be. My eyes are playing tricks with me. Gloria wiped her specs.

The lass jumped into a sparkling turquoise pool. Water splashed right through the screen and onto Gloria's face and hands. A drop of moisture glistened on the tip of her finger.

Translucent and lovely in the warm light. And there, inside the tiny capsule, was a man doing somersaults. He looked oddly familiar.

She gaped. 'It's Big Brother. But how shrunken and powerless he is.' She laughed. I'll never be afraid of you again, Vance.

The image faded. Cool metal stirred, in the palm of her hand. She gasped. There glittered a shiny new sixpence.

Potted

Mike's the name. Feel a squillion dollars, rolling up to the party at Fred's old semi-detached video shop. Splurged on my outfit. Imported silk shirt – two hundred bucks. New pair of flares, Extra shine on my shoes. A splash of Stud aftershave and I'm ready. Boy, am I ready.

This one's his second business. Another's just down the road. Fred's reeling in the moola, let me tell you. Can't wait to see a bit of the action.

I've been employed here since he started. Any day, any time, any shift. Good old reliable me. He's starting a third shop. It's a cert the boss will put me in charge. I'll be happy as manager – for a while. Then I'll branch out on me own – not that I plan to tell Fred.

I jumped at the chance to help with Debbie's, eighteenth birthday party. Who wouldn't? His daughter's quite a chick. Thinks she's too good for the likes of me. But, after tonight, I reckon she might sing a different chanson.

Wait until she sees my new wheels. The latest Range Rover. I'm proud the way I squeeze into the last parking spot. 'I've Got My Mind Set on You', a George Harrison number, blares from my radio. I hum the tune. Shivering at the possibility of having Deb in my arms. I see specks of dust on the bonnet. Wipe them off with my handkerchief.

I head for the house. 'Dancing with Debbie' seems to vibrate from every weatherboard. Birthday girl's not in sight. I put my gift with the others. Her favourite Billy Joel numbers. I'm dying to see her reaction.

Pop music from the band. Guitar, keyboard and drums, friends of Deb. I fight my way through pink balloons. Blinded by strobe lights. Catch my head on the banner emblazoned, 'HAPPY 18th, DEBBIE.'

It's gonna be a great evening.

Couples shriek, laugh and gabble. Grandpa's singing along to Billy Joel's 'This is the time'. He raises his beer and gives me a wink. I return a thumbs-up. Great old bloke.

The boss dances with his missus. Rosie isn't in bad shape for an old bird. Blonde hair all piled up. Cleavage almost to her waist. Must've been a looker in her day.

Young ones can't stop giggling. They swig cups of punch, non alcoholic. You'd swear it was laced with something stronger than ginger ale. Wouldn't put it past young Brian. A handful, that kid.

The boss grins at me. Bald, belly spilling over his belt. Black shirt drenched with sweat 'Great to see you, Mike. Hand out the sausage rolls and sandwiches, will you?'

'Sure, boss.' I pass around the trays of food. Pour booze for the oldies. Don't touch a drop myself. Gotta stay sober. Fred's depending on me.

But where's Debbie?

Granny overflows from a wicker chair. Floral dress, cheery grin. She's sipping a shandy. 'Thanks for helping, Mike.'

Groups of the youngsters keep disappearing out back. Granny peers their way. 'All this coming and going. What are they up to?'

'Good question.' I chuckle. 'Maybe smoking pot.'

She wobbles with laughter. Figures I'm joking.

It's odd, I think. The action's in here. I slip out to take a look. Hear the cackles before I see their glazed eyes. Smoke rises from their funny cigarettes. In my day (and that's not so long ago), a fag behind the dunny was about as daring as it got.

Should I tell the boss? Not sure how he'd handle it.

Young Brian sidles up. Seventeen, going on eleven. Proud of the six hairs sprouting on his chin. Cocky little bugger, just got his licence. God knows how.

He grins and jangles a bunch of keys. 'You left these in the ignition.'

I grab them. 'Thanks.'

His furtive glance. A whisper. 'Mike, I just moved your Range Rover. Had a bit of a prang. Don't tell Dad, will you?'

'You what?' People know me as a gentle bloke. Cool it, man, cool it, I think. 'What do ya mean? A bit of a prang?'

'Backed it into Tony's car.'

I gulp. 'Tony?' He's built like a rugby forward, with a temper to match. 'Is it badly...'

'Nah. Only a scratch.'

Thank God. My hands ache to grab Brian by the scruff of his neck. March him up to Fred. But would the boss see it my way?

It's then that I glimpse Debbie. A jolt in my guts. She's kissing some pimply youth. Miss prim and proper would have some explaining to do if Fred caught her making it with that loser. The idiot hasn't even had the manners to put down his joint.

I picture running my hands through Deb's crinkly golden hair. Pert boobs against my chest.

Deb looks up. Anxiety in her eyes, she rushes over. A change from being ignored. The touch of her hand burns my forearm. 'I don't smoke dope myself, Mike. Honest. Don't tell Dad.'

I clear my throat. Suddenly hoarse. 'You should know me better than that, princess.'

Her smile would melt the ice caps. 'Thanks, Mike.'

Her lips brush my cheek. I'm mesmerised. But Fred's calling.

He looks grumpy. 'Where the hell were you, Mike? Need another case of beer. And more ice for the punch.'

I'm itching to nick out front and check the damage to my wheels. But the jobs keep coming. The band plays 'Don't You Forget Me' by Simple Minds.

Debbie cuts the cake. Everyone sings 'Happy Birthday'.

Presents glitter on the table. She opens them to squeals, laughter and cheers. A cursory glance at mine, before she rips the wrapping from another one. I blink.

Fred makes his proud father speech. A good one, but far too long.

Debbie blushes throughout her response. It's over in minutes. No sign of the boyfriend. I feel a surge of hope. She'll dance with me before the night's over. But suppose I ask and she refuses? Make me look a right dill. Still, she owes me.

Rosie cuts the cake. Piles it on an enormous platter.

I ask, 'Shall I fetch another?'

'One's fine, Mike. A strong lad like you. It'll be empty in no time.'

I stagger around the room. 'Do have some cake, folks. Take a napkin.'

The band is playing 'Every Breath You Take', usually one of my Billy Joel favourites. Now, it makes me uneasy.

Oops. Tony's heading my way. Clenched fists, face puce.

I force a grin. 'Cake, mate?'

He ignores my question. 'You own that green Range Rover?'

I smile, glowing with pride. 'Sure do. New last week.'

'You bastard.' He's almost frothing at the mouth. 'I borrowed a car for the party. You've cracked the bumper, broken the headlights. Crumpled the bonnet.'

I gulp. 'Hang on, there. I didn't... I haven't...'

'It's obvious you backed into me mate's car. Why deny it?' Tony takes a swing.

I duck. The punch misses. But I lose balance. The platter hurtles towards the floor. Horrified, I watch the cake scatter in slow motion. Folk step out of the way, collide. Breathing hard, I consider my options. Tony's past listening. And if I tip young Brian in it, how'll that sit with Fred?

Guests slip on the polished floor. Shoes garnished by cream and cake. I back away. Someone stumbles against me. Beer cascades down my front. Might be funny, if it weren't so darned serious.

Rosie drags a mushed handful of icing and chocolate from her cleavage. Shrieks, 'Clumsy oaf.'

It misses me by inches. The crowd jeers, whistles, claps. 'On ya.' They make a space, ready for the fun.

Fred barges towards us. 'What the hell's going on?'

I glance his way. In that millisecond, Tony's knuckles crack against my nose. God, the pain. Blood pours down my face. Drips over the front of my shirt.

My rage erupts. It's a shock, even to me. I take a mighty swing. Bruise my hand against bone and solid muscle.

Tony grabs my shirt. The fabric rips all the way down my back. We slip and slide on that bloody cake. Before you can say silk shirt, we're wrestling on the floor. I must've blacked out.

Someone told me it took four blokes to prise my hands from Tony's throat. I open my eyes, find the bunch dragging us apart.

Debbie sobs. 'You moron. You've ruined my party.'

Fred's eyes bulge. 'What the hell got into you?'

'Boss, I swear I've done nothing.'

'Look at yourself, Mike. You backed into Tony's car and it isn't even his. You'll damn well pay the damage. I asked you here to serve drinks, not get pissed.'

'I haven't touched a drop.'

He sniggers. 'Tell me another. Smell yourself.'

I keep my trap shut about the pot. Say nothing about who moved the Range Rover. Apologise. Swear it won't happen again.

If youse hear of any jobs…

Pop-up Author

A new kind of book will soon hit the shops. No, not a Kobo or Kindle or any sort of electronic reader. This one boasts a POP-UP AUTHOR. It will make critique groups, editors and mentors obsolete.

A reader feels the beginning is too long. Pages of description, while the protagonist stands on a chair, a rope around his neck?

The POP-UP AUTHOR shouts. 'You numbskull. Description sets the scene? Try harder.'

Drowning in purple prose? The author dwells too long on her darlings? You keep skipping pages to find some action?

POP-UP AUTHOR screams. 'Get used to it. I spent hours at my computer sweating over this. I'll not delete anything for the sake of you or the book.'

'But –'

'No buts, buster. It's my most creative work. Read every word. Or else.'

So you, poor shivering reader, plough on.

You fail to understand a certain chapter, phrase?

POP-UP AUTHOR sniggers. 'Idiot! My cousin twice-removed thinks it's a gem. You've 350 pages yet to read.'

Characterisation gone awry?

POP-UP AUTHOR glares. 'Everyone else thinks my protagonist is perfect. The secondary characters are good too. What's wrong with you?'

You dare to question some metaphor?

POP-UP AUTHOR raps you across the knuckles. 'That's the way I see it. What's your problem?'

Historical allusions sprinkled like currants through every line?

POP-UP AUTHOR sneers, 'That's my style. Read the classics. Muddy, convoluted style?

POP-UP AUTHOR, outraged. 'My mother says it's wonderful.' Ending doesn't work?

POP-UP AUTHOR folds her arms. 'You just haven't got it, have you? Nothing but trouble throughout. Oh, why do I bother?'

So next time you buy a book, check between every page. POP-UP AUTHOR could be hidden there, waiting to pounce. Good reading!

Death Drive

Walt drove with caution, holding forth about politicians.

Zelda added the occasional 'Yes, dear,' or 'No, dear.' Accustomed to his rants.

The next moment, her husband slumped over the steering wheel.

She went into shock. 'Wake up, darling. Walt…' Gosh, another mini stroke. Knew I should drive.

The van shot forward. Made it through a green light. Sped along the highway.

Walt snored on.

Zelda's mind raced. The ignition key and brake were out of reach. 'Walt!' Her scream brought no response. She tried to shake him awake.

He moaned, but didn't open his eyes. Walt was a solid man, so she couldn't move him.

The vehicle mounted the footpath. It missed half a dozen posts on the grass verge. Zelda trembled. Who'd have thought our lives would end like this? Let's hope we don't take some poor soul with us.

Her voice grew hoarse from shouting. It felt as if she were watching some madcap Mack Sennett movie. Funny, if it wasn't so darned serious.

The van zoomed around a corner, slicing its way between trucks, cars and a motorbike. Her mouth lost every drop of moisture.

Let the end be quick…

The vehicle tore round in circles. Zelda gasped, clutching the grab handle. They took a right, crossing the highway a second time. By some miracle, they dodged another pack of traffic. Shot forward, bumping up onto the footpath.

The van mowed down a line of small trees. Slowing by increments. Came to rest against the last but one. The engine roared.

Walt woke, looking around. 'W…what the devil are we doing here?'

'You may well ask.' Her anxiety gave way to hysterical laughter. 'Turn off the ignition. Nobody will believe me…'

An ashen face appeared at the driver's-side window. By a million to one chance, their son, Rory, had stopped to have a flat white at a small café nearby. 'Mum, Dad. Are you all right'

Zelda wiped her eyes. 'Pinch me. Tell me I'm alive.'

Walt slumped.

Zelda groaned. 'Not again.'

'Sit in the back, Mum. Rory hefted his father into the passenger seat. Strapped him in. 'I'm taking you both to the doctor.'

Walt blinked awake. 'Why are you driving, Rory?'

'It's a long story, Dad. Sit tight.'

Walt made a crablike entry into the surgery. Hemiplegic after an operation for a brain tumour, decades earlier. His one good hand manipulated cameras, loaded film. Using the useless one as a prop.

Walt chatted to the doctor in his habitual imitation of good cheer. 'I'm fine, doc,' he said. 'Fine.'

The doctor's jaw dropped at Zelda's tale. 'As they say, truth is stranger…' He checked Walt's heart and blood pressure. Examined Zelda. Shot Rory a glance. 'It's a miracle. Not a scratch.'

'Shall I take Dad to hospital?'

'All that poking and prodding would just make your father feel worse. Walt, rest in bed. Your transient ischaemic attacks – mini strokes – are getting worse.'

'Doc, I'm OK.'

'Walt, be good.' Zelda frowned. 'Doctor, there's just one question…'

'Driving?' The doctor shook his head. 'Walt, promise me you'll let your wife take over the wheel.'

'But, doc, I'll be fine. Give me a day or so…'

'Fraid not, Walt. It wouldn't be worth the risk. But I do recommend one thing.'

'What's that?'

A cheeky grin. 'Buy a million dollar lottery ticket. Given your luck, you're bound to win.'

Charlotte's Sleepover

The sun shone high in the afternoon sky. In the mellow golden light, Charlotte drove up for her sleepover. Travel bag on wheels, Wiggles sleeping sack and sleeping mat. It needed no pumping, but would require a gymnast to roll it up after use.

Charlotte's mummy said, 'She finds it more of an adventure to sleep on the floor, rather than in a bed.'

'Fine. Saves me changing linen.'

My granddaughter danced with impatience. 'You can leave now, Mummy.' Keen for us to be alone, so we could dress up in our finery. 'We'll put all our jewellery and dresses and stuff on your bed – is that a good idea?'

She unrolled a little mauve party dress with a pink sheen. I'd snaffled it in Bath, and liked the rose decoration in the same silky fabric. Longed to see her wear it.

Charlotte checked the matching attached petticoat. 'I'll need help with the buttons and sash.'

I laughed. 'Everyone needs a lady-in-waiting.'

'Can we get dressed now?'

I guessed my granddaughter had been looking forward to this occasion for days. 'Let's get everything ready for our special dinner first.'

We passed through French doors to the garden room. Charlotte liked my pink tablecloth and rose-patterned napkins. She added the cutlery, while I put out the side plates. We arranged the glasses – tall, plastic ones. I suspected she was too young for crystal.

A tour of the garden yielded bright pink geraniums and pink ladies.

'Now can we put on our things, Granny?' She showed me her watch, necklace, ring and sparkly shoes.

I slipped on my regalia. Charlotte had chosen a violet in crinkly cotton with a long, full skirt and sash. She eyed my necklace. Ten strands of tiny beads, with iridescent purples, greens and pinks, and three huge faceted pink glass beads joined by silver fixings, spaced at centre-front and either side.

'I love your necklace, Gran.' Her tiny fingers caressed it.

'A present from a friend. I couldn't possibly give it away.'

Her blue eyes sparkled. 'Then can I have it when you die?'

I laughed. 'Barring traffic accidents, that may be a while. But when I go, the necklace is yours.'

My granddaughter also put in first claim for my Italian shoes and dresses. 'I'll be big by then and able to wear them.'

Charlotte did a pirouette. She exulted in the swirl of her skirt. 'Spin, Granny. Spin around.'

I gave a half-hearted whirl.

'Your skirt is so lovely and long. Faster, Granny, faster.'

I giggled. 'Time to stop. I'm giddy.'

We toasted each other in mango juice. Jess, her once-fluffy white cat, was our a third guest. Silent, grey and bedraggled, she wore red beads, and handmade satin and lace dress.

Charlotte gagged over my chicken vol-au-vents. I should've stuck with the bought Angus beef pies, which we both like. She enjoyed bread roll, potatoes, carrots and greens. Had no appetite for the mango and ice cream dessert. I made up for her. We listened to gurgle of fountain music from my pond. Gold light played over the leaves of the bird's nest fern and yellow-green robina stirred in a gentle breeze.

She called home, making sure all was well. Mummy and Daddy were surprised to hear that we'd already eaten. She was worried about her brother. Poor fellow had come down with chickenpox, too young for the injections. He was excited to hear his sister's voice and tried to grab the phone.

It was too early for bed. Charlotte's eyes sparkled. 'Let's go to the park in our pyjamas.'

'I don't think so, sweetheart.' I laughed. 'We'll change into play clothes.'

It was a delightful afternoon, still bright – why hadn't I brought a hat?

Charlotte made a new friend, Ellie, a year younger than herself. Her daddy gave both girls a high start on the swings. Played a game of hide-and-seek.

Ellie was disgusted when her father hunkered down behind the bar-becue. 'You should've hidden behind the trees.'

He laughed. 'Then you'd have found me even quicker.'

It was time for Ellie to go. We made our farewells.

The ritual of pyjamas and teeth-cleaning.

Charlotte had a new plan. 'We can go for a walk to the park at six o'clock tomorrow morning. Then have another dress-up for breakfast. Is that a good idea, Granny?'

I took a big breath. 'It's a great idea.'

She yawned. After several stories, I made to turn out the light.

Charlotte had a sudden worry. 'What if you die in the night? Then I'd be all alone.'

'Call Mummy and Daddy's number. Or dial 0 three times. Tell them Grandma won't wake up.'

'Good idea.'

She dozed off in her sleeping bag.

Sometime in the early hours, the creep of a small body wriggled into my bed. A few months earlier, she'd have been rushing me up at first light. Now happily content to cuddle while we had a conversation about Mummy, Daddy and Ethan.

Seven a.m. Charlotte took me to the park. We found it deserted, save for the early warble of a magpie. She soared high into the sky on the swing. Squealed delight on sliding down a slippery dip. I helped her collect leaves and other objects for paint-printing.

Breakfast over, she called home. Cooing and squealing to Ethan. No doubt, he was pleased to know she was still around.

We made ready for painting. I persuaded her to wear one of my old T-shirts over her good play clothes. 'To keep them clean.'

She squeezed a tube of poster-paint. 'No, no. We have to break the seal first. I'll take charge of this.'

Afterwards, Charlotte watched *Play School* and other kids' programs on ABC TV.

I seized the opportunity for deep breathing and meditation.

We explored her repertoire of games. Hide and seek. Monsters. Chasings. She giggled over a gobbledegook conversation. Neither of us knew what the other person was saying but it made for heaps of laughter. Came the moment for roaring around the patio on the trike – her, not me.

Milk, cheese, biscuits and chips made a perfect morning tea.

She sat on my knee. I told her the story about the boy who cried wolf. It raised a lot of questions.

After a game of *Thomas the Tank Engine*, she kept asking, 'Is it time yet for Mummy and Daddy?' She couldn't hide her excitement over her next engagement: a play afternoon with her friend Jasmine. Keen to tell Mummy, Daddy and baby Ethan of her adventures.

My Sister Florrie

The mare galloped back, riderless. Bridle broken.

Father shouted, 'Florrie should never have been allowed to ride that horse alone. What were you thinking, Aileen? A mad animal like that.'

My elder sister burst into tears. 'She wanted her turn.'

Father tore up Dry Creek road. Returning, ashen-faced. Florrie limp in his arms. Someone screamed. Only later did I realise it was me. I'd have done anything to shut out the terrible wails, moans and laments.

Mother trembled. 'My baby! Oh, my baby.'

The following days were a blur. Muffled sobs issued from Mother's room. People moved quietly around our house, not wanting to disturb her.

Only Father attended her funeral, as men did back then. Her name was never mentioned again. We didn't want to upset Mother and Father.

But I couldn't stop thinking about my little sister. My favourite playmate. Numb in those first days, later grief and loss. The pain was almost unbearable. I ran and ran. Anything to stop the tears.

The shop lady saw me running one day. 'Why are you running so fast, Joe?'

'So I won't cry for Florrie.'

Mrs Beckons gave me a musk lolly, trying to be kind, I suppose. I could never bear the taste of it afterwards.

I've never forgotten Florrie's laugh. Even as a baby, she chuckled, her whole world a joy of dances, play and fun.

In dreams we ran hand-in-hand, my sister and me.

We visited a place where once we played, only better. So many flowers, brilliant colours, an intensity of blue, yellow, red. I'd never seen such glory before. Those in Mother's garden weren't half as bright. We met under the bluest sky I'd ever seen. For the first time since Florrie died, I felt a sense of peace and tranquillity.

'Don't cry for me, Joe. I'm fine. We'll meet again some day.'

The vision faded. Though I woke to tears, they were tears of happiness.

I couldn't tell anyone about my strange experience. Nobody would believe me. Besides, I didn't want to upset them. I didn't know where she was buried. And Father didn't believe in visiting graves. It no longer mattered. Knowing she was somewhere safe, sure I'd see her again. Hadn't Florrie said so?

Knight in Shining Chain Mail

A chill London breeze whipped rain against Liza's trousers. Her shoes squelched with every step. Twilight had swiftly descended. Totally lost, she took the map out of her pocket. Checked her location. None the wiser.

The tube strike had complicated matters. It should have been a cinch to meet Emma at Paddington station. Earlier that morning, the walk had been easy.

Swallowed by mist and darkness, she felt sick with anxiety.

Buses disgorged commuters. They rushed by, clearly keen to be home out of the drizzle. Some ignored her pleas for directions. Others had no advice to offer. She dodged puddles, turning this way and that. Close to panic.

Liza darted into a hotel. Blurted out her problem.

The desk clerk grinned. 'The Bakerloo line is still working, luv. That'll get you there. It's just along the way.'

Liza entered the tube at Oxford Circus. Relief palpable, she took a seat in the train. Almost light-hearted, she thought, why did I worry? Passengers left and entered. The next stop was Paddington. She readied to alight.

The train whizzed past her stop. Liza felt devastated. I've no choice but to get off at the next station. But how on earth will I find my way back in the rain and darkness?

An inner voice consoled her: you'll be all right.

She exited the barriers. About to consult an official in uniform.

He began giving directions to a tall, handsome young man with the same problem. 'Ten minutes walk and you'll be at Paddington station.'

The stranger scored his map with a pen.

Dare she hope he was a knight in shining chain mail? Not an axe murderer?

Liza asked, 'Do you mind if I tag along?'

A warm smile. 'Not at all.'

The pavements gleamed. Wet in car headlights. They negotiated a twisting confusion of streets. Ascended a bridge over disturbed waters. Followed a path beside the lapping ripples of a canal, gleaming with coloured images of city lights. It seemed odd to be sharing her adventure with a total stranger.

'The name's Liza – I'm visiting my daughter in Bath. She's a painter – just finished her Masters in Fine Arts.'

'I'm Luke. What a coincidence: I'm an artist too. Did my Masters but I'm now working in commerce. Love painting but it doesn't earn enough.' Luke was running late for a dinner engagement.

Ten minutes walk became fifteen, twenty…

Light spilled into the pools of rain outside a pub. Liza's knight seized the opportunity, asking a passer-by whether they were on the right track.

Reassured, Luke pointed towards a large building. 'That's Paddington station.'

Liza thanked him profusely. 'I'm pleased to see that even in the twenty-first century, chivalry is alive and well.'

He laughed, and bowed. 'Have a good evening.'

Guest of Honour

Jane gazed with dismay at the glowering skies. 'I wanted to serve tea in the garden.'

A posh Hampstead patch, every branch and leaf dripped. The plastic table had sagged. Raindrops dimpled the pool therein.

But Jane wasn't about to be put off by saturated undergrowth. 'It's stopped. Let's stroll around the garden.'

The British stiff upper lip and all that, I thought. And dreaded ascending her algae-coated steps. Australians give our guests the right to choose. Nana Jane's words carried the power of a Royal Command.

We trod sodden paths. Thin soles of my shoes squelched.

Jane lifted the head of every drooping plant. 'This one's growing like Jack's beanstalk.' Another had barely survived the winter. 'Isn't this purple flag iris a picture?'

The Lady in the Bath revealed her charms. A dock in her wild corner thrived.

'Smell the roses.'

Shivering in the English summer, I waxed enthusiastic. Rain had diluted the scent.

'And look at the fruit on this espaliered fig.' A vine from next door threatened the climbing rose. 'The little man who used to prune it has died. Doesn't do a lot any more.'

I thought, he wouldn't.

The sky puffed out gloomy cheeks. Drips away from another downpour.

My hostess clapped her hands. 'Let's risk the garden for afternoon tea. We'll wander around, cups in hand.'

I daren't voice any doubts

Raindrops struck at the heart of every leaf. Falling fast. Faster. We made it down those treacherous steps and indoors, without a second to spare. I sank gratefully into a comfortable chair.

Jane wrung her hands. She agonised over cruel fate which had once again put the garden out of bounds.

About then, Naomi, my daughter, and her family arrived. She and Daniel hugged me. Chloé embraced Nana Jane. But she took a step back at my approach. In Australia, a year or so back, she'd been all hugs and smiles. A stage, I thought. Children are absolutely honest. My first grandchild, ditto Jane's.

The other evening, Chloé had declared, 'I love Mummy and Daddy. I love Nana Jane. I love Pa. I love Durga. But I don't love Ganma.'

Durga, her aunt, looked triumphant. Jane gave a pleased little smile.

My daughter took her aside. 'Darling, that wasn't nice. Grandma loves you very much. She's come a long way to see you. You must be polite, even if you don't love her.'

Our hostess assembled the cups for afternoon tea. She forgot the milk. Spilt the sugar. I feared she might be exhibiting the first signs of dementia. But a later chat with someone who'd known her in younger years, convinced me she had long been…well, different.

Durga was sixteen when her mother asked whether she had yet enjoyed pleasures of the flesh.

Durga had flushed, answering in the negative.

'Why ever not?'

Jane served chocolate cake, and scones. 'Homemade.'

Daniel's handstands of appreciation had Naomi and me sharing a bemused glance.

Jane declared. 'There's one slice of chocolate cake left. Would you or Naomi like it?'

I didn't hesitate. 'Yes please!'

Jane plonked the cake on my side plate. 'Oh! You're having it, are you? I meant that tomorrow for my morning tea.'

Another quaint English custom? I devoured it with relish.

Jane scanned the sky. 'Hardly a drop. Let's go.'

Naomi smiled. 'Count me out.'

Daniel's eyes bulged. 'Don't argue with Mum.'

'I'm not arguing,' Naomi said. 'I'm staying here. Enjoy yourselves.'

Chloé played with Daniel's old toys.

Daddy asked her, 'Do you want to go into Nana's garden?'

The child coughed. Shook her head.

Naomi said, 'Just let her be, Daniel. Best she stays indoors with that cold.'

He left. Blinking.

Nana Jane looked distraught. 'But Chloé loves my garden.'

'Yes, Jane,' I said. 'But look how happy she is here.'

Jane's disappointment informed my decision to join them. Ritual admiration of her garden is a family duty, I mused, circling the soaked paths, with all the enthusiasm of a caged tiger.

The rain dripped back. I offered a silent prayer of thanks. Stalking indoors, I picked up a volume of short stories.

Jane spied my book. 'Where did you get that?'

'From the shelf.'

'Be sure to return it to the same place.'

I gritted my teeth. 'Yes, Jane.'

We sipped our glasses of red. Daniel's sister, Durga, arrived.

Jane announced, 'Time to put the rolled piece of pork in the oven.'

It looked the right size to serve two guests. Our party was six.

She glowed with pride. 'You wouldn't dream the trouble it took me to debone and stuff it.'

I grinned. 'Well done.'

Daniel charged our glasses. 'It's stopped raining.'

Durga, Daniel and Jane grabbed their Merlot ready for another viewing of the garden.

Naomi and my decision brought blinks of disapproval. Low mutters.

Jane said in a voice designed to cut through steel, 'If you're comfortable, of course you can stay indoors. But – are you sure?'

'Yes, Jane. We're perfectly happy.'

Daniel said, 'Come along, Chloé.'

Naomi stormed, 'The damp's not good for a sick child.'

His shout, 'Fresh air will do her good.'

A chorus of 'It's not wise to coddle children.'

Against a backdrop of saturated undergrowth, the adults posed, glasses aloft. A tableau of wine, flowers and disapproval. Chloé, bright as a butterfly in her rainbow-hued jacket, charged between dripping plants.

A shower took them by surprise. They hurried back.

Durga spat recriminations. 'It's perfect out there. So cool and fresh. Perfect.'

My daughter and I shared rebellious chuckles.

Jane announced, 'Supper, everyone.'

We took our places.

'Daniel,' said our hostess, voice imperious, 'I want you to carve.'

He made to open the wine. 'Naomi, you do it.'

Naomi took up the carving knife and fork.

Jane glared. 'What are you doing? I asked Daniel to carve.'

'He's busy, so…'

'Oh! I'll do it myself.' Jane shot me a proud glance. 'I bought this pork from the farmers' market. Do you have those in Australia?'

'Oh, yes.'

There was barely a slice of pork per person. Chloé's plate remained empty.

Jane said, 'Each of you give the child a little meat and vegies.' She served the vegetables.

Grateful to be the guest of honour, I received three beans, a minute portion of broccoli, a tiny portion of peas. And one small baked potato.

Durga and Daniel scored rather better in the beans and potatoes department. Chloé grizzled. Stern words from her parents. She devoured offerings from our plates in a trice.

'Nana, may I haver more meat?'

Jane frowned. 'There isn't any, I fear. Have some potato.'

Wine flowed. We'd recently visited Bilbao. My hopes of discussing the wonderful Guggenheim Museum and fabulous paintings never made it past Jane's garden.

I gratefully accepted a second potato. Fearing it might be another faux pas.

Jane apologised for the bought pudding. A delicious steamed cake with currants, glacé cherries... 'Should we wait or have it now?'

'Now will be perfect, Mum.' Daniel finished the last of Chloé's peas.

The cake was served with ice cream. We all agreed it tasted yummy.

Our hostess asked if I'd be free the following Wednesday? 'We could have tea in the garden.'

I expressed profound regret. I'd seen enough of her mini Kew to last me the rest of my days.

The Indian Tea Man

Dad tackled dangerous mountain roads with aplomb. Had taken the tiring journey to town countless times. But that radiant afternoon, his whistle betrayed anxiety.

Mum, Dad, Druce and I occupied the front of our five-ton Bedford truck. In the days before mandatory seatbelts, my sister Vivi rode on the back. She sang Buddy Holly songs at the top of her lungs.

Our father treated the vertiginous incline and hairpin bend ahead with caution. And I wasn't the only one to breathe a sigh of relief to have that section behind us. It had claimed a number of victims, including the Indian Tea Man and his brightly painted van. The pedlar had been remembered not for any achievements in his life, but for the manner of his death, long before I was born. An accident doubtless pondered at length. Had it evolved from a miscalculation of speed? Or did loose gravel conspire in his fate? His exotic origins had ensured the tale a permanent place in local myth and legend.

The truck groaned along in low gear. My legs tensed against the floor.

Daddy crouched forward, gripping the steering wheel, like a lifesaver. 'My God. No brakes.' He frantically pumped the pedal. Pulled on the handbrake. Saying, 'It could never hold a large vehicle. Not on a steep pinch like this,'

The Bedford began to gather speed.

Soon it will take off, I thought. Like some mad, uncontrollable animal. The tyres slewing in the gravel. Jolting and bouncing. Turning over. Flinging everyone out. Or crashing on top of us. Smashing our bodies on rocks and logs.

At seventeen, I felt cheated. My life would be over before it had begun.

The terrible note in Dad's voice made me shiver. 'I've only one chance. Put her into this tree.'

The truck hurtled towards a small eucalypt. Time slowed. Seconds twisted into hours. I watched my last moments unfold. Darkness gobbled me whole.

I'll never know how long I drifted. Unconscious. Then my eyes opened. Amazed to find myself alive. I recalled nothing of the impact. Heard a dizzy, ringing sensation. Perhaps I hit my head.

Druce moaned, clutching his knees.

Dad flung open the door. Deathly white, he jumped out. Rushing around to check on Vivi. He helped her down from the back. Bright blood ran from a wound on her nose. He wiped it with a clean handkerchief.

'Nothing serious, thank God. Thought we'd all bought it.' He inspected the damage. 'Water leak, large dent in the core.' Daddy whistled. 'Engine's been displaced at least an inch.' Dad shook his head. 'Any more speed and that small tree would never have saved us.'

Vivi told me, 'Just before the crash, the theme of a popular song spun around in my head, It was crazy. Crazy. Just a crazy dream.'

I shivered. 'If only.'

The first on the scene was a local vicar, on his way home from a distant parish. 'Nobody badly hurt? Thank the Lord for that. Can I drive you somewhere? Sorry, there won't be room for everyone.'

He drove Dad, Mum and Druce to their cabin at a nearby road site. A river diversion project.

Our vehicle sat at an angle, partially obstructing the road. Vivi and I directed drivers past it, nervous over the responsibility. Relieved to glimpse our brother, Victor, driving the Ferguson 135 tractor. He made short work of towing our truck out of harm's way, before tootling off again.

The scent of eucalypt hung on the warm air. Somewhere a kookaburra laughed. We felt overjoyed to see Cousin Polly's FJ Holden drive up.

She chuckled. 'You girls will do anything to get a bit of publicity.'

We laughed. 'So it's our fault?'

'Of course.'

Polly's gift of friendship helped to overcome the shock of our near-miss. We toasted sandwiches in her jaffle iron. Jokes and laughter entertained us far into the night.

She grinned. 'Heard about the fellow who said to his girlfriend, "Let's get married or something." Her response, "Let's get married or nothing."'

We fell about laughing. 'Who thinks of these gags?'

Poppy gave us both goodnight hugs. 'You've been spared for a reason, girls. The Indian Tea Man wasn't so lucky.'

Undertow

Marisa smiled. 'Shaz! Great to see you again.'

Air kisses.

'Let's start with a Bollinger.'

A long hug.

'I've set a table up in the garden.'

Shaz eyed the pink roses in a crystal vase. Matching serviettes. Delicate bone china, silver tea service. Giggled. 'You always did know how to party.'

The cork squeaked. Pop. Liquid foamed into tall crystal.

Marisa clinked glasses. 'To us.'

Shaz giggled. 'Best friends. Where did all those years go?'

A sweep of lawn rolled down to Wild Goose Bay. Vistas of snow-capped peaks. Tall grasses waved to rhododendron and birch. Nymphs peeped from behind a burbling fountain. The aroma of wallflowers mingled with the salty tang.

Shaz sighed. 'Gosh. What a stunning outlook. I can't wait to see the interior of your house.'

Marisa heard her own bright voice, as if from far away. 'Marvellous architect – took advantage of every view.' A nervous laugh. 'Noisy neighbour, so Taylor bought the place next door.' Why am I extolling his brilliance? Truth lurked, driven by the undertow. 'Fancy a tour?'

'Thought you'd never ask.' Sharon's eyes widened at the indoor/outdoor pool. Acres of gleaming marble. Cathedral ceilings gave way to walls of light. The paintings... 'Gosh, Marisa. You have everything.'

'You might say that but...' I daren't tell her. Why break the spell?

Best pals until Sharon and her family moved away. The last time they'd met had been in the final week of high school. And now, Marisa had received an invitation to the Brookfield High reunion. She hesitated. Should I accept?

Taylor had sneered. 'What will you have in in common? It's been decades.'

I can't bear his controlling behaviour, she thought. 'I plan to go, Taylor.'

On the night, he had glared. 'What time will you be back?'

Marisa grabbed her coat. 'Don't wait up.'

Shaz arrived late. Their eyes met across the babbling table. Intervening years melted away. Shaz had chuckled over her almost non-existent wrinkles. Run a hand through her tangle of grey hair, eyeing the blonde perfection of Marisa's coiffure. 'I've never been brave enough to tint…'

'Nonsense, Shaz. Just do it.'

The night sparkled with nostalgia and laughter.

'You married an eminent surgeon, Marisa? Four kids. Wow.'

If only she knew, Marisa thought. 'And you, Shaz?'

Sharon beamed. 'Twenty-year anniversary last week. Three beautiful kids . Not much else. But I love Laurie to bits.'

Marisa tried to recall the loving Taylor of their early days. Reminding herself that the kids and grandkids adored him. 'Wonderful, Shaz. Congratulations.'

'Not famous or anything, like your Taylor. A carpenter. Meant to get his own business but…'She shrugged. 'We've almost paid off our little home. Laurie fixes stuff weekends.'

'Good for you, Shaz.'

They exchanged emails and addresses. Arranged a meeting. Marisa thought, who could have predicted the horror that unfolded yesterday?

Too late for a cancellation.

Outside, they clinked champagne glasses.

Shaz brought out old photos. 'Gosh, look at us in kindergarten, holding hands. Big bows in our hair, missing teeth.' Shaz giggled. 'We told each other everything.'

Seconds ticked by. Marisa hardly dared breathe. The moment passed.

Sunshine glittered from every wavelet.

Shaz said, 'It's your very own resort. 'Wouldn't dare ask you back to my little cottage.'

'Taylor wanted this huge place. I'd have been happy in some quaint little cottage.'

'Sweetpeas and hollyhocks around the door?'

'Something like that.' A voice whispered, just tell Shaz. Marisa daren't risk the humiliation.

Shaz sipped freshly brewed tea. Spread a scone with strawberry jam and cream. Patted her tummy. 'My diet starts tomorrow.'

Bright sails criss-crossed the spangled bay.

'Must be a fairyland out here in the evening.'

'Pleasure boat operators point out where we live. Extol our lifestyle.' She thought, why did I say that?

Sharon brushed back her unruly hair. 'So it's one big holiday all year round?'

'Actually, we have a place up the coast.' A brittle laugh. 'Taylor likes to…to surround himself with acolytes. Generous host. Urbane, witty. Fourteen friends for a long weekend.'

A grin. 'Gosh… One big party.'

'And your vacations, Shaz?'

'We save all year. Mum minds the kids. We snuggle up in a motel, just the two of us. Laurie likes to fish, so off he goes in a hired skiff. I settle back with a good book. Lazy swims and moonlit walks along the beach. Different restaurant every night. The one time we splurge. Probably sounds dull to you.'

Marisa thought, what I wouldn't give for that. 'You know, Shaz, people get through a lot of towels in four days. Heavy sheets. Often the washing machine breaks down. Taylor won't spend on maintenance. I seldom stop cooking, shopping and cleaning.' She thought, tell her that's far from the worst of it.

'Shall I get to meet the lovely Taylor?'

'No, it's his evening out with friends.' And by the time he's home I'll be long gone... 'Another champagne?'

'I shouldn't but... Your life is exactly as I imagined it. Even down to the *maison secondaire*. We buy lottery tickets.'

They clinked glasses. 'Here's to the Big One.'

Shaz giggled. 'Shouldn't tell you this but...Laurie knows exactly how to please a girl. You know, in bed. I'm so lucky.'

Marisa stiffened. Snap! The stem and bowl of her champagne flute parted company. Drops of blood mingled with Bollinger.

'A flaw, I guess.'

'Gosh, your lovely glass. Why, you've cut yourself.'

Marisa blotted the wound with a tissue. 'It's only a scratch.'

Shaz glanced at her watch. 'Oops, must rush. Got to pick up my kids.' Adding, 'Don't even look at our old Beetle. It's such a wreck.'

Marisa said, 'So long as it gets you around.' She hadn't meant to sound patronising.

A bise on each cheek. Mmn, Mmn. One long embrace. Marisa wiped her eyes at the thought that they'd be unlikely to meet again.

Night after night, Marisa had delayed going to bed. Hoping Taylor might be asleep. His rituals became intolerable. The video revolution fuelled new torments. She'd suggested he consult a psychiatrist.

Taylor sniggered. 'Counselling's only for idiots. You have the problem.'

Outrage. Pain. How could she take her kids from their father? Even now that they were adults, with families of their own, she daren't destroy their illusions.

The crisis point had arrived yesterday. Marisa returned home early. Surprised to find all the downstairs shutters closed. Hairs rose on the back of her neck. Entering noiselessly, she found Taylor crouched over the TV screen, like a rat. Gloating at the sight of women being muti-lated. She had backed away, gagging. Luckily, he hadn't seen her.

Marisa drove around for hours. Struggling to process this new horror. Stopping the Beamer, she threw up. Rinsing her mouth from the water bottle.

I need my clothes and other stuff, she thought. It's one more night here, risky as it may be. I'll host Shaz tomorrow, then make my move.

She had returned home, jangling her car keys. Gave Taylor time to hide the evidence. Ignored his guilty face. Stilled the tremor of her hands, pouring him a red. 'How was your day?'

Taylor had left for work as usual that morning. Marisa stowed her cases in the boot of her BMW. No doubt he'd cast himself as the victim. Her the foolish wife, suffering a midlife crisis. Silence was the price she must pay to protect her family. Friends would be shocked by her desertion. She could hear them even now, A shame. Such a lovely man.

After waving Shaz away, Marisa changed her outfit. She'd already booked a motel. Trembling, she slipped into a blue silk blouse. Ignoring the ache from tender, dark bruises on hidden places of her body. Some were faded and turning yellow. Never again need she submit to Taylor's sick games. She closed the zipper of her navy skirt.

Picked up her keys and handbag. Took a last glance around. From now on, all communication will be through my attorney.

A movement caught her eye. God, no, no. It's him. But, why…

Light glinted from a scalpel blade. Her heart raced. In that millisecond of terror, the doorbell jangled. Her assailant stopped short.

Marisa clattered down the stairs, two at a time. Flung open the huge front door.

Two earnest-faced Jehovah's Witnesses waited on the porch. 'We'd like to talk to you about the Bible.' They stood, open-mouthed, as she ran right on past.

The key shook in Marisa's hand. It took her three attempts to insert it into the ignition. She gunned the motor. A shriek of tyres spat gravel. Her Beamer roared off into the fading light.

Trout

School holidays found me confined to my room. Sniffles had brought blisters. Scabs turned into pimples.

Mum applied calamine. 'It's chickenpox. Don't scratch.'

'Oh, why can't I play outside?'

'You're infectious. We don't all want to get the jolly thing.' She held up my red plastic whistle. 'Stay in bed and you may have this.'

My favourite toy. Never before had she allowed me to blow it indoors. The delight of placing it to my lips and blowing it almost made up for bodily discomfort. Hour after hour, a high-pitched screech reverberated throughout our house. Poor Mum. How did she bear it?

Days passed. I played that jolly whistle to my heart's content. But, by then, a strange thing had happened: I shuddered away from my toy's plastic taste. And the piercing whistle brought back every itch. I couldn't wait to toss it into the bin.

A fishing holiday in the Mount Royal ranges promised to be just the medicine needed after such an ordeal. My honorary Auntie Violet and her son, Shorty, Daddy's best friend, joined our party.

A keen fisherman, he was well over six feet tall. I couldn't understand why adults called him Shorty. Auntie smiled, 'His nickname is just a joke, dear.'

Shorty's elderly father, Uncle Jim, stayed home to mind his khaki Campbell ducks. He wore a built-up boot and walked with a limp.

It fascinated me the way those birds tipped back their heads to sieve food. Uncle also kept caged canaries. They sang beautifully. He whistled along, in perfect harmony. But I felt sad to see birds locked in cages. Daddy used to say they should be left to enjoy their freedom, soaring through open skies.

Auntie Violet chuckled. 'This is a wonderful opportunity for adventure, girls. I love the bush.' She planned to take us on long rambles. 'Birdwatching is such fun.'

We pitched camp near the Gummi River. We three girls shared a tent.

Auntie Violet gave tips on comfortable camping. 'I've read it's a good idea to dig hollows matching the shape of one's body. Makes an excellent base for sleeping bags.'

Using Dad's pick, we dug away clods of grass. Hers was plump. Mine tall and thin. Vivi's small and chubby.

Before bed, we watched the men make fishing flies. They tied bright feathers to each hook. 'Trout think these are tasty insects.'

Clever, but sneaky, I thought.

I settled down for the night, cosy in my sleeping-bag. Somewhere in the forest, a mopoke spoke his name. I could scarcely wait for the night to be over. Then the fun would begin. Auntie blew out the lantern.

My eyelids closed. Next moment, something odd woke me. I heard grumbles from the others too.

Auntie said, 'My hat. What was that?' She grabbed her flashlight. 'Well, I never. A mini avalanche of loose earth. It's tumbled into our bedrolls.'

Every movement increased the volume of soil encroaching on our spaces.

Auntie shared the story of the princess with a pea in her bed. 'She'd never have coped with this.'

We laughed. But not for long.

No sooner did I drift off, than one of the others cried out. Giggling, we joined forces to throw hellish lumps of soil and pebbles out of Vici's bed. Then Auntie threshed around. Another earthen invasion. Giggles became groans. Then came my turn to seek help.

It seemed the longest night of my life.

Wide awake at first light, Auntie helped us move the tent. She glanced at the diggings. 'A pity we didn't have some seed potatoes, girls. We'd grow a perfect crop.'

Somewhere, a kookaburra laughed. I couldn't even raise a smile.

Everyone teased us over our plight.

Shorty grinned. 'Told you it would never work, Mother.'

Auntie did well to join in the laughter.

Our first ramble took us deep into the rainforest. Willy-wagtails danced. Robins flashed their red breasts. The song of a thrush enchanted us all. We shuddered away from hairy sawfly larvae. Spitfires clustered in twisting bunches on eucalypts branches, waving their mustard-coloured heads.

Tiny, criss-cross ripples flashed shimmers of sunset across a pool in the river. I sat on a tussock, knees tucked under my chin. Frogs croaked in the swamp.

Shorty warned me, 'Be very quiet and still. Mustn't frighten the fish.'

Red and blue dragonflies darted, dropped and rose in the golden light. A whipbird practised his call.

Shorty cast his line. He flicked a feathered fly across a pristine pool. Before long, his reel whirred. The line spun free. A trout sped off, fighting to escape. Daddy came to look.

Shorty's eyes gleamed. 'It's a whopper, Joly.'

It took an age before the struggle stopped.

Shorty grabbed his landing net. 'Sure glad I brought this.'

Dad eyed the pretty spotted fish. 'A meal for all of us.'

The poor creature wriggled and gulped for air. My excitement faltered. I wiped my eyes.

Shorty put it out of its misery.

Daddy patted my shoulder, 'I know how you feel about killing such a lovely creature. But it is for food.'

Shorty longed for a set of scales. 'The biggest trout I've ever caught. What do you think it weighs, Joly?'

'Must be at least six pounds – if not more.'

Shorty grinned. 'After a beauty like this, I'm happy. Even if it's my last catch on the trip.'

Daddy shook his head. 'Don't put a hex on yourself, mate.' He rattled stuff around in the back of our truck. Found a wire contraption to cook the trout. One he had fashioned from fencing wire, and carried on trips, 'just in case'.

Our family gathered around a leaping campfire. The grilling aroma made me ravenous. There is nothing quite so delicious as freshly caught trout. Moist and pinkish in colour like salmon, Mum served it with corn on the cob, baby potatoes and damper.

Dad dropped a handful of tea leaves into bubble of water. Banged the billy side to help them settle. I loved the mingled aromas of gum-leaves and smoke. The tea had a unique taste too.

Shorty yarned of all the big ones that got away. Dad told of fishing in other rivers. Eels longer than your arm, of gudgeon and perch.

Aunt Violet winked. 'Never believe fishing tales.'

Leaves whispered secrets only they could understand. Clouds drifted by, painted in red, yellow and purple. Shadows chased away the mellow light.

A wallaby edged forward on front paws and elbows. Stopping now and then to nibble sweet grass. Kookaburras joked in the gold-drenched eucalypts. Sunset turned to twilight. The first stars blinked in the dark sky.

The red glow of dancing flames.

Shorty refilled the billycan from Dad's canvas water bag. 'I feel like another brew.'

Daddy lit the lantern. They yarned into the night of gold-mining days, and nuggets the size of boulders.

I yawned. Struggling to keep awake.

Auntie sighed. 'Men! Dreaming of Eldorado.'

Next day, Vivi developed spots. Mum took one look. I gulped. 'Oh, no! Chickenpox.'

Dad set my sister up in her own tent. 'You're ill. Stay in there.'

She popped out every few minutes, spots and all. Giggled and played. Mum didn't seem amused. But nothing could persuade her to stay put. At last, she fell asleep. Everyone breathed a sigh of relief.

Mum raised her eyebrows. 'Thank goodness.'

The plangent cry of a dingo. I burrowed deeper into my sleeping bag. Comforted by Auntie Violet's steady breathing.

Shorty became the next victim.

Aunt Violet chuckled. 'Not a sign of any chickens, son, but more than your fair share of spots.'

Nobody laughed for long. Shorty's fever soared. And, it seemed, lesions appeared all over his body. Some even turned up in his mouth and hair.

We packed picnic baskets, tents and fishing rods. Shorty looked a ghost of himself.

Dad put mining dishes into a corn bag. 'Shorty's words were prophetic. Guess he wasn't meant to catch another trout.'

Not Her Time

Violet said, 'I'm not afraid of dying, you know, sister. It happened to me once.'

'Tell me about it'

'I collapsed at home.'

'Did you see anything while you were unconscious?'

'Oh, yes! I went to the most wonderful place you could ever imagine. Walked in a park with blue and white flowers. A lovely, glowing light transformed everything into the most vibrant colours you could ever imagine. I saw my mother as a young woman. My father looked older than her. Everything was relaxed and peaceful. I didn't want to come back. But a voice said it wasn't my time.'

'Do you recall returning to your body?'

She shuddered. 'It was horrible. They used those paddle things with jolts of electricity. Resuscitating me brought back all the pain. It took me a while to recover. Then I learnt that my niece was getting married. I offered to make her wedding gown. It was a lot of work but made me very happy. Her mother had died of cancer when the children were very young. I'd promised to do what I could. To think I was able to create something special. The bride declared my work exquisite. "Your designer gown made my day."'

My Stars

I'd met Perrie on a tour of Scotland. Twin room, shared excursions. Within days, we laughed over tales of old boyfriends, husbands, divorce, widowhood and much more. Adventures, families, problems and achievements brought us even closer. It seemed I'd known her forever.

It amused us the way tour husbands seized the smallest opportunity for a flirt. Their wives briefly absent? Extravagant praise ensued, of our outfits, perfumes and personalities. We chuckled at their audacity. Flattered nonetheless. Our journey laughed all around that bonnie country, onto the Orkney Isles and back.

Our trip ended on a high. A drive around Tassie beckoned. A hired car, shared expenses. Our friendship didn't miss a beat. Next time I looked, we'd known each other for twelve years, without a cross word. Laughing over the same jokes. We played the fool, with exuberance.

One shop lady asked if we were gay. Probably the baseball cap I wore gave her the wrong impression. We didn't tell her to mind her own business. Laughed our heads off.

I wiped my eyes. 'No, I'm a merry widow and she's a gay divorcee.' Perrie insisted I buy a girl's hat.

A second Tassie trip. We planned to visit Bothwell, on the east coast, for a Spin-In. Then explore the west coast. Not that I spin or weave but Perrie does, and do I like craft. Late in the organisation, Perrie asked if one of her spinning group pals could join us. What could possibly go wrong?

Verruca seemed pleasant enough. Protruding teeth, receding chin. Nobody can be blamed for their appearance. We shared gales of laughter, giggling like teenagers. But the long-suffering girl in the next room at the youth hostel banged on the wall: she had to be up at dawn the following day.

We moved to a farm-stay for the Spin-In week. Verruca and Perrie did the same courses, so went around together. Not surprising, given their common interest. More often than not, I found myself wandering around the exhibitions alone.

About then, Perrie began challenging my every remark. She reminded me of a sassy teenager, rebelling against a parent. Cited certain of my idiosyncrasies. 'You are funny, aren't you?' She had failed to notice my failings previously.

Verruca lurked nearby with that toothy, knowing grin.

Perrie said, 'You do have ideas about everything, don't you? I suppose it's because you're a writer.'

I thought, that's a problem?

Verruca sniggered.

Perrie couldn't decide whether a pretty orange and yellow six-strand necklace might be a bit over the top.

'Well,' I said, 'if that's your worry, you could remove one strand.'

She glared at me. 'I don't want to remove one strand.'

Verruca smirked.

Disagreements took wing, accelerated. *Persona non grata*, I scarcely dared to open my mouth. Perrie's behaviour made no sense. Until then, we had shared nothing but harmony. I had secretly nicknamed Verruca 'the Chipmunk'. Guessing she gnawed away at my character, behind my back. The only explanation for Perrie's sudden change of attitude. I wondered at her motive. Jealousy? A personality disorder? Or both?

The Chipmunk confessed to being a loner. A state of affairs which often results from behavioural issues. Only one thing remained clear: a warm friendship had soured.

Dinner preceded a concert.

Perrie announced, 'Verruca and I are tired. We plan to go back to the house after our meal.'

My jaw dropped. Why hadn't they discussed the issue with me, before making it a fait accompli? I had paid my share of the car hire, so should have been consulted.

Perrie compounded her folly by rushing to consult a couple of other ladies. They boarded at the same farmhouse as us. 'Are you staying for the concert? Could Dessie have a lift home?'

I seethed. She made me feel like a piece of unwanted baggage.

Dinner over, the Chipmunk made a miracle recovery. She remained throughout the evening. The entertainment proved superb. Excellent songs and band. Jokes that had us all chuckling.

We returned to our lodgings very late. Despite earlier exhaustion, Perrie was wide awake, knitting.

The Chipmunk flew home early the next day. Never had I felt happier to see anyone leave. Hoping that my friend's attitude might improve. But Verruca's poison carried an aftertaste: Perrie's unpleasant remarks continued.

She worried about getting a parking spot close to the backpackers.

'I'm sure we could find one around the block.'

She scowled. 'Don't want to park there.'

I commented on the excellent laundry facilities.

Instead of a yes, or I've seen better, Perrie snapped, 'Oh, I don't plan to do any more washing until I get home.'

Pleeese! Give me a break.

Perrie had become teetotal. I missed a celebratory drink with my meal. Not that we had much left to celebrate. But going to bed early every night wasn't my idea of holiday fun. The journey brought no respite from her negative attitudes. Laughter had degenerated into jeers.

Back home, Perrie rang. Oblivious to her bad behaviour, it seemed.

Recent back problems gave me an idea. I told her of my non-existent bad back, and my supposed horoscope predictions. 'A person you have recently met seems genuine but is making critical remarks behind your back. This woman is trouble with a capital T. But you have a secret advantage: a friend will come to realise the truth.'

I joked, 'Wish whoever is doing it would get on their bike. My back's playing up something awful.'

A long silence. Followed by, 'Really?'

Seemed to confirm what I'd already suspected.

Perrie went into a long monologue about what she had been doing recently. Seemed preoccupied. Was her mind busy with the big question. 'How does she know we've been talking about her? Did she overhear something?'

Perrie told me how badly treated by a friend she'd been during a recent holiday in Queensland. Her 'challenging every remark' had a familiar ring.

Poetic justice, I thought, hiding my chuckles.

Perrie arrived chez moi, exhausted, following a drive from the mountains. I asked had an accident fouled up the flow of vehicles? Someone's bad driving upset her? But no. Made me realise how stressed she feels over normal traffic.

'How about dinner at Top Ryde this evening?'

She spent a good half-hour perusing the street directory. It puzzled me. I meant to navigate, and knew the way.

In darkness, we returned to her car. Perrie searched, not knowing how to turn on the lights. I was astounded. Twelve months, and she hadn't driven it at night.

Perrie challenged and second-guessed my every comment or suggestion. Our laughter of former years was missing in action. She needed a bed each time her car was serviced. But our friendship was no longer under warranty.

Plead Guilty

The member for Willawong brushed back silver hair. Seated in a worn leather armchair at his home office, he shook his head. Was it only this afternoon when he, Richard Carson, had sauntered with such easy confidence along the eastern corridor of Parliament House? Greeting colleagues. The capped perfection of his smile. Pats of encouragement. He'd be around for a while yet.

The press had howled for his skin. A campaign almost hysterical in its vitriol. I run the party, not some blasted newspaper, he thought. Certain members juggled for his position. But Richard never doubted he had the numbers. Never noticed the signs.

One last whisky before the vote. Toasting himself in advance. 'To victory.'

The vote had come close. Damned close. Some of those he had counted on for support… 'Good luck, Rick.' They'd said. His gracious speech conceding defeat had been the hardest of his career. Emotion took him by surprise. That photograph would grace the front pages of every tabloid in the morning. He dreaded the thought.

TV crews jostled for interviews, shoving microphones into his face. 'Do you support the new leader?'

'Absolutely. Wish him all the best.' He couldn't begin to count the damage their stories had done in the weeks leading up to the spill. The fake respect in their voices made him want to puke. 'If you'll excuse me, gentlemen, I have to go.'

Politics. A dirty game with an irresistible attraction. The most exciting years of his life. But, now, he thought, it's time for my wife. A new start.

In the days before mobile phones, he glanced at the wall telephone.

'Should I call Serita? But why bother? The evening news will be full of it.'

He selected a few small items. Mementos of the last thirty years. Photos of Serita on their honeymoon. A crystal paperweight. Put them in his Italian leather briefcase. His staff would sort out the files tomorrow, get busy with the shredder. He glanced around the office, shrugged.

Serita greeted him in the drawing room. 'It's on every channel. Sorry, old thing. The back bench?'

He cleared his throat. 'Actually, I've…uh…' A politician lost for words. Richard eyed her gleaming black hair, swept up into a new style. An emerald necklace highlighted the colour of her eyes. Dressed to celebrate, he thought. Her beige gown caressed every curve. He longed to take her in his arms… It had been a while.

Serita reached for two antique crystal glasses. Red nails, beautifully manicured.

Richard swallowed. 'It's game, set and match. I've had enough.'

'Sorry.'

They had kept up a united front in public, of course. His wife was a perfect foil to his mature charm. Her painting by Gavin Williams hung above the Carrara marble fireplace. A splendid likeness. He could never decide what it was about the darned thing that made him uneasy.

Serita picked up the tongs. Clinked in ice. She added the whisky. 'So… You'll no longer need a token wife.'

Until now he hadn't realised… I still love her. 'Darling, I thought a holiday…'

'Together?' Moisture glistened on her long lashes. 'This charade hasn't been easy for me, you know.'

He downed the drink. 'My dear Serita. I'd hoped…'

'I stayed while you were in parliament. That was the arrangement.'

Richard took the decanter and poured a double.

She hesitated. 'Gavin Williams and I plan to…to…'

'Marry? He laughed 'That young pup? Can't be a day over twenty-five.'

Anger flashed in her green eyes. 'What's age got to do with it? He loves me.'

So the rumours were true. 'You're over forty,' Richard said. 'Do you imagine he'll want you in ten years?'

'A decade of love will be better than nothing.'

'Nothing?' His eyes bulged. 'This is the best house in Willawong.'

'I was happy before we bought this…museum.'

Richard glanced at the painting. Now he knew what disturbed him about the damned thing. The expression in her eyes. The way she used to look at him. 'Your affair has…'

'Ruined your career?' She laughed. 'You've managed that yourself.'

'At times, I might have a few whiskies too many. Who hasn't?' He lapsed into silence. Shadowed with the dread of empty days and lonely nights. Somehow, he must get her to see reason.

A clock chimed.

Serita assumed her hostess smile. 'You'd better change for dinner. Our guests are about to arrive.'

'Tonight? Surely not.'

'Arranged weeks ago. Remember?'

Richard crashed his empty glass onto the table. 'Make my apologies.'

He strode into his study. Slammed the door. Poured himself another drink. Slumped down. Where had it all gone wrong? Scholarship boy. Grammar school, summa cum laude at university… It was no surprise to anyone when he married the lovely Serita Henning. Ah, those happy days before life got in the way of love.

Memories crept back. Friends had invited them to a rifle range. Serita was a natural. Hit the target every time.

'Darling, you're amazing.'

She'd laughed. 'I learnt to handle guns as a kid at my family's place. Back in the country.'

Music and laughter issued from the drawing room. Serita was one loss he could never accept.

He had set his sights on the seat of Willawong. Endorsed by an overwhelming majority. Serita backed him at every step of his rise and rise. Spent a lot of time away from home, with parliament sitting. He'd thought she understood. Politics came first.

He had ignored the rumblings of discontent in the party. Even after the disastrous results of the last election, the criticism of his leadership. Why change his style now?

Someone even had the temerity to suggest he curb his drinking. Boy, did I give him an earful. The whisky bottle was empty.

A discreet knock. Damn. Must be the housekeeper, he supposed. Helping out with the dinner. She knows I don't like being disturbed. 'Yes?'

The door squeaked open.

He noticed something vaguely familiar about the face. Richard blinked. 'Who the devil are you?'

A smirk. 'Gavin Williams, sir.'

Richard swayed to his feet. 'How dare you come to my house.'

Gavin laughed. 'I'm Serita's guest, sir. She's asked you about divorce?'

'Go, you fool… Before I have you thrown out.'

Gavin sniggered. 'Surely you've had enough bad publicity?'

Richard clenched his fists. 'Stop seeing my wife…'

Gavin lowered his voice. 'Sling me a few grand…'

Richard felt a pounding in his temples. 'I guessed you'd have a price.'

'You rich old guys make me sick. Can't even screw your wives and keep them satisfied.'

Richard took a swing. His knuckles smashed against bone. Gavin went down. Lay motionless.

'Get out of here, blast you.'

Gavin remained still. Too still. Richard's heart battered against his ribs. My God. I haven't… He probed for a pulse. Found none.

Ice pulsed through his veins. Go, he told himself. Leave before it's too late. The bungalow. That was the answer.

Richard crept out the back way. The motor of his Porsche purred into life. It would never be heard above the thump of the band.

It took a supreme effort to concentrate on the shadowed freeway. Red reflectors warned him not to stray over the edge. He drifted towards a concrete barrier. Headlights from another vehicle warning, not a second too soon. He jerked the wheel, regained his lane. Whistling to keep himself awake.

At the property, he breathed in the aroma of cypresses. Recalled their honeymoon in Italy. All those years ago…

Richard stumbled through the moonlight. The effort it took to shove his key in the lock. His shoes crashed to the floor. He collapsed into bed. Snoring before his head hit the pillow.

Afternoon sunlight poured through the bedroom window. He stirred, shocked to find himself at their holiday cottage. Disgusted to be in bed, fully dressed. Oh, his throbbing head.

Moments later, it all rushed back. He rubbed his bruised knuckles. Foolhardy thing to do. Wouldn't have happened if I'd been in my right senses. Not that I'm sorry the little mongrel is dead.

He glanced at his watch. One p.m. Odd the police haven't tracked me down by now. Serita must have found Gavin long ago. She'll be heartbroken. It's foolish to expect a telephone call.

He noticed that the receiver was off the hook. Let the damn thing stay there, he thought.

The cops should arrive at any moment. A squad car would swing up the driveway and the member for Willawong – the ex-member for Willawong – would be driven off. Well, they weren't going to find him unshaven.

A blunt razor took nicks out of his skin. It felt good to see a few drops of his own blood. God, that cold shower felt good. Helped to sober him up. Richard downed two Panadol. Who cared if they were past their use-by date? Like me, he thought, with a wry grin.

He put on a fresh shirt and trousers. Hands shaking, he knotted his tie. Slipped into his jacket. Brewed a cup of instant coffee. Milk powder. It tasted dreadful.

Richard sat in a wicker chair. Waiting. With a supreme effort, he ignored the bottle of whisky on the sideboard. The new me. Please hurry, he thought. I want to be taken sober.

Richard sighed. I should call my solicitor. Affected by alcohol, that would be his defence. Might get off on a manslaughter charge.

Strange the constabulary haven't arrived, he thought.

A motor sped along the road. Funny, there's no siren. In cop shows, there's always a siren. And flashing lights. He closed his eyes. Imagined the cloud of dust furling among the eucalypts and cypress.

A vehicle screeched to a stop out front. Just one? Where were the others? Richard groaned. For once, he hadn't prepared some clever speech.

Footsteps hurried along the gravel path. Crossed the veranda. The front door burst open. A woman with dishevelled hair stumbled towards him. Gray slacks. Suede jacket. Ravaged face.

'Serita, darling. You…'

'Richard. Thank God. Thought you might be here.' She flung her leather driving gloves onto the table.

He licked his lips. 'It wasn't planned, I swear. Gavin came to my study…'

Her eyes widened. 'You spoke to Gavin last night?' There was an edge of hysteria to her laughter. 'He left the house without a word.'

Richard flooded with relief. Gavin's alive, he thought. Thank God. He babbled. 'You…you mean…I'm not a killer…'

'I phoned him this morning.' There was a bitter nuance to her voice. 'You were right.'

Richard's career might be over. But he still had Serita. 'Sweetheart, forget Gavin. We'll make a fresh start. I'll go to AA…'

She seemed calm. Too calm. 'When I rang, a woman answered.'

'There were bound to be others.'

'Gavin came on the line. Said he'd never loved me. Laughed. "Cop it sweet, honey bunch."'

'Forget him, darling.'

'I wanted to hear him say it. Face to face. Gavin came to the door in a towel. Big bruise on his chin.'

'I did that.'

A pallid smile. 'Water was still running. Her, in the shower, I guess... Planned to give him a fright... Your pistol, hidden under my coat.'

He froze. 'What?'

'Took it from your desk drawer.' Serita trembled. 'He called me a silly bitch. It was all about money. Something snapped.'

He face-palmed. 'No...'

She shuddered. 'I'll never forget Gavin's expression. The...the thump as he...he fell. His blood...'

'Did anyone see you leave?'

'The girl was still inside. Yelling her head off.'

'And the...the pistol?'

'M-maybe I dropped it... Ran to the car.' She wept.

'It's all right,' he said and held her close. 'I love you, Serita. Always have.'

A squad car roared up the drive. Red and blue lights flashed. A siren wailed. Two doors slammed shut. Two pairs of footsteps scrunched along the gravel path.

Richard saw her wide terrified eyes. The last vestige of colour drained from her face. He squared his shoulders. 'Drive yourself back to town, darling. I've a feeling it might be a while before I'm home.'

Let the Fun Begin

A joyous arrival at Bath. Hugs and kisses. At three, my grandson, Josh, had reached the territorial stage. Wary of strangers. Likely to provide challenges over any attempts at familiarity. I decided on the best way for an Aussie gran to bring down the barriers: ignore him.

Within a week, intrigued, he came to me.

My daughter, Naomi, grinned. 'Let the fun begin.'

Dining room chairs became train carriages, Josh the driver. We emerged unscathed from terrible crashes.

Playing the monster became one of his favourite games. He giggled with delight when Granny screamed. Siren noises from a battery-operated car had Gran hiding under a baby blanket. More giggles. He joined me, bringing all his friends for protection.

I clutched an armful of teddies, dogs, dollies, monkeys, snakes…

Josh also adored hide-and-seek. Like the majority of children, the game never failed to bring giggles and delight. I moved around his bedroom, while he hid, wriggling, under a blanket.

I pretended to be oblivious to all that movement. Padding right on by. 'Now where can that boy be?'

My grandson couldn't stifle his chuckles. If my search took too long, he would shout, 'I'm here! I'm here!'

During sessions with his model train, I declared, 'It's impossible to fit batteries into such a small space.'

The three-year-old was delighted to show Granny how to insert them.

He made imaginary dishes, with ingredients ranging from snakes to poison and dog poo. 'Now, my wife, we must make some soup.' He instructed me, 'Be a cow or sheep. Make moo and baa noises, Gran.'

Josh also loved being some 'aminal'. He ordered me to become a dinosaur model, whatever that might be. Gave instructions on appropriate mouth movements. The voice had to be just right. Sometimes I got the correct intonation.

He said, 'Gran, I love my skelenton shirt.'

I said, 'Well, there are bones just like that, inside all of us.'

He laughed at the absurdity of such a notion. 'Nooo! I don't have bones in me.'

We read his favourite stories.

Our shoes carried on imaginary conversations, adopting all sorts of silly voices. He giggled at our little plays.

I minded him when his parents went out. Giving voice to one of his plastic dinosaurs, I used an appropriate tone of sympathy. 'You'll be all right, Josh. I'm here.'

His separation tears stopped in seconds.

Once, he declared, 'You can't mind me. I'm not your auntie.'

Patterns on the inside glass doors distorted my face into multiple images. Often, the sight of that was all Josh needed to become calm again.

Once, Mummy slipped away. Inconsolable, he sobbed all the way upstairs. Heading straight for the corner where Mummy read his nightly stories. He comforted himself by reading one of his regular stories.

On a good day, Josh could count to twenty. He enjoyed playing number games. The little boy had very sensitive feet. Socks had to be smoothed just so before he put on his shoes. He had a good eye for matching colours and liked to choose his favourite outfits. Ones not always appropriate for the weather.

Once, he needed to be pushed outside the front door in his undies to convince him that warm attire might be appropriate.

Naomi reminded me, 'A similar thing happened with Chloé, around the same age.'

Josh found it difficult adapting to transitions. A spirited child, his fussing over food aggravated adults. We craved to relax and enjoy Daniel's delicious meals.

I had a brainwave. 'Why not give him a pep talk just before he sits down at the table? Remind him of his expected behaviour.'

Naomi warned Josh, 'No complaints are allowed over your chair, plate, spoon, glass, drink, or the food... Understand?

He nodded.

These reminders proved amazingly effective.

One night, adults enjoyed a special treat – fresh asparagus.

Josh hovered.

I knew how he hated being excluded. I said, 'Josh doesn't like green stuff.'

Normally, he rejected anything of that colour.

Indignant, he said, 'I do like green stuff.' He gobbled down a whole piece.

Everyone laughed.

At a popular fish and chips café, the portions were more than generous.

Naomi asked for a spare plate. 'I'll share with Josh.'

He glared. 'I don't want your chips. I want my own.'

Naomi took away his plate. She hid behind a low wall, pretending to ask the waitress for different food.

Sauce was already squeezed on the plate, so I didn't think he'd fall for it.

Happily, Josh ate the meal without further ado.

A Flair For Flower Arrangement

At the coach station, Anna took a great breath.

Forrester said, 'You mean to go, then?'

Anna nodded. He's always believed I'd change my mind, she thought. The first time I've defied him in years.

'Be careful what you say.' He brushed back thinning hair. 'Don't shame me in front of Kitty.'

A peck on her cheek.

Anna wiped the spot, stepping aboard. Secretly, she felt ambivalent at the thought of meeting Kitty, her husband's precious niece.

Forrester gave an uncertain wave.

Ten days of freedom. It had barely sunk in yet. Thank goodness the latest bruises, on her neck, had almost faded. Make-up covered the yellow discolouration.

She opened her old leather handbag. Studied a faded photo of Kitty, a plump young woman. Taken shortly before her wedding. One of the boys, barely more than toddlers back then. Mark must be twelve by now, young Alan ten.

Her only vacation had been a lifetime ago. She had splurged Mother's small legacy, visited England. Met Forrester. All charm and bonhomie back then. Made me feel a special girl in some romantic fantasy.

Did Forrester only propose because I was pregnant?

The birth of her sons, Joe and Peter, then two miscarriages. Forrester's brooding silences made her uneasy. Arrival of Emma, their daughter, made the one bright spot in that difficult time.

Bleak English winters and damp summers took their toll. She yearned for clear Australian skies, the scent of gum leaves on the hot December air.

Forrester suggested emigration. 'A new start will do us both good.'

He found employment. 'You get us a place to stay.'

Confined to a small hotel room with three children under six proved a nightmare. Drawing books and crayons helped to keep them occupied. Walks proved good exercise for young legs, and made them tired.

Emma cried at night. Guests banged on walls, complained to management. Forrester grumbled over disturbed sleep. Anna paced, the baby in her arms. Emma finally asleep, Anna slipped, exhausted, into bed.

A young girl minded the children. Anna trudged from one estate agent to another. Garish carpets and lurid wallpapers stared her down. Some places were cramped; she couldn't breathe. Reasonable prices brought the lingering odour of too many curries.

A spacious garden flat at Honeysuckle Bay had just become vacant. Close to shops and a small park, and only minutes from the school, it seemed perfect. On sunny days, Emma slept peacefully under an old liquidambar tree.

Her choice initiated a major row.

Forrester shook with rage. 'Why, for Pete's sake, did you take the first place on offer? The one above has sweeping views of the lake. All we see are blooming clotheslines.'

'The other one was twice the price.'

She trekked around finding furniture. Forrester offered no help. Then grumbled over the outmoded settee and oak table setting, bargains for a few dollars, second-hand. He disliked the roomy but inexpensive wardrobes. They lacked the money to buy better.

'What would one expect from someone born in the Colonies?' Forrester sneered.

He caressed the lid of his Challender piano, crated and shipped at great expense. Played with a cold, mechanical dexterity. It set her teeth on edge.

Anna fabricated falls to explain bruising or a black eye. Ashamed of her guilty secret.

Forrester was contrite. 'Don't know what came over me. It will never happen again.'

At first, she believed him. Three kiddies and no money. Where could she go? Did she have a right to deprive little Emma and the boys of a father?

Forrester's promising career in marketing stalled. 'My salary's only a fraction of what a man of my talents and experience might expect. A first class honours degree, yet they gave Mallory the promotion. It's your fault.'

She gaped. 'Mine?'

'Companies take wives into account. And addresses. Trust you to rent on the wrong side of the bay.'

'You could try working for a different company.'

'How dare you! A high school dropout. Telling me what to do.' He glared. 'It's time you got yourself a job.'

'I like to be here when the boys arrive home from school.' Among her greatest pleasures were their cries of greeting each afternoon. Tales of the lads' achievements. Drawings and stories. 'We'll manage.'

'Manage? Just like the rest of your family, no ambition. If only you were like my niece Kitty.'

Anna could have recited it off by heart. Orphaned at an early age. Self-educated. Perfect marriage. I should hate her, Anna thought. But Kitty writes such cheerful, friendly letters. Invites me to visit.

Her chums joked, 'Your hubby sucks all the oxygen out of a room. You could cut the tense atmosphere into cubes.'

Everyone laughed. But it wasn't funny. They arranged to call when Forrester would be absent.

Anna decided, I'll make him proud of me. With her kids at high school, she took WEA classes. Everything from philosophy to ancient history and Greek.

Forrester sneered. 'Lightweight.'

Their daughter, Emma, married her young man from the air force, moved interstate. Not long afterwards, Forrester picked one of his many quarrels with Joe and Peter. Before the day was out, they had packed their bags. Vowing never to return.

Anna wrung her hands. 'Where will you go? What will you do?'

'Work our way around Australia.' They hugged her, tears in their eyes. 'You don't have to stay you know, Mum. You've put up with him for too long.'

Later, Forrester's eyes blazed. 'It's your fault the boys left.'

She said nothing. At least he did the dishes. Now and then.

Anna took a part-time job at a florist's shop. Discovered a flair for flower arrangement. Secretly, she put aside money each week. Once, supplementing her funds with a couple of hundred dollars lottery win. She took in ironing. Minded children. Within a year, she had accumulated well over two thousand dollars. And growing. A lifesaver should she need to leave.

She felt unwell. Headaches and episodes of muddled thoughts.

The doctor diagnosed high blood pressure. Prescribed tablets. 'Take a holiday. It'll do you the world of good.'

About then, Anna received Kitty's latest invitation. She weighed her options. Afraid of travelling alone. Yet I went to England by myself, she thought. But that was before Forrester.

He laughed at her suggestion. 'You won't accept, of course. I wouldn't want Kitty embarrassed by someone of your limited intellect and education.'

Something snapped. 'I am going.' Anna felt surprised at her own audacity.

'And how, might I ask, do you propose to fund this little jaunt?'

She hated his smirk.

'You're not using my Bankcard.'

Her voice was quiet. 'I have my own money.'

Forrester blinked. 'But…but… Who'll make my meals?'

'I'll freeze you some casseroles.'

She splurged. New wardrobe. Swanky suitcase. French perfume. I'm not about to be shown up, she thought.

Anna delighted in the wide Australian skies. Tantalised by the red landscape. Glimpsed kangaroos and emu. Crows feasted on road kill. Reluctantly flapping away as their vehicle rumbled past.

The coach made regular stops to let off passengers. Passed lonely hamlets. Clusters of untidy buildings huddled beside the highway. Freedom had already worked its magic. The other passengers enjoyed Anna's company, and she theirs. Anna laughed more than she had in years. Perhaps I'm not stupid, after all.

Wonderra. A small outback town, miles from anywhere. It reminded her of a Russell Drysdale painting. The sole person to alight, Anna stepped out into merciless heat. She clutched her hand luggage. Waiting in the shade of the coach while the driver retrieved her suitcase from the luggage compartment.

The vehicle rumbled away. Engulfed by blinding light, she popped on her sunnies. All part of the adventure. Kitty must be running late.

A dusty cab prowled.

Anna told the driver, 'I'm being met.'

He dipped his sweat-stained Akubra and drove away. She welcomed a few minutes to compose herself.

But where was her niece?

Kitty's place is close to the coach stop, she recalled. The wheels on her heavy suitcase rattled over potholes. Hot and sweaty, Anna asked directions from a service station attendant.

'Clairvaux Street? Second on the left. Can't miss it.'

Anna struggled up the slope. Neat front yards, tidy houses. Palms and tropical trees. Just the sort of street she'd expected. She stopped to catch her breath. Wiped perspiration from her brow.

Number 31 loomed into view. She looked twice to confirm the sighting. Paint peeling weatherboards. Uncut grass. An old mattress. Her head ached. Trust me to get it wrong. Kitty's place must be number 13. She dreaded that trek back. Darn this heat.

At that moment, the torn flyscreen door swung open. Banged shut.

An obese woman with unkempt grey hair and bare feet plodded her way. Face vaguely familiar. 'There you are, auntie. Must've drifted off.' A sloppy kiss. 'Lovely to see you.' Pale eyes gleamed at her aunt's expensive clothes. Drifted to the new suitcase. 'Come on in out of that heat. Make yourself at home.'

Anna's eyes bulged. She stepped inside a room that smelt of dogs and stale urine. Two black German shepherds clawed at Anna's slacks, woofing loudly.

'Get off, you mongrels.' Kitty's kicks sent them yelping away.

Anna felt her head spin. She eyed discarded clothing, toys and *True Romance* magazines.

'Say hello to your great-aunt, boys.

Mark and Alan barely glanced up.'

Kitty glared. 'I told youse boys to call me so's we could meet the bus. Sorry about that, auntie.'

Anna's voice almost failed her. 'Coach coming tomorrow?'

'The bus? Nah. Once every ten days.'

Kitty cleared a space on the sofa. 'Sit down, auntie. You must be all in. Cuppa?'

Anna slumped onto the seat, numb with shock and dismay. 'Th-that would be lovely.'

Kitty moved towards the kitchen. Excess kilos wobbled under thin fabric.

Kitty poured tea into chipped mugs. 'Milk and sugar?'

'Uh… Black will be fine.'

A loud vroom, vroom outside.

'That'll be the lovely Freddo.' Kitty waved from the window.

A hippopotamus of a figure sat on a huge black motorcycle. Removed a shiny black helmet. Red face and scraggly beard.

'Handsome bloke, isn't he?' Kitty chuckled. 'Lucky me.'

Anna bit her lip. I dare not laugh or I'll cry.

Fred dragged a fag from his mouth. 'Good to see you, baby.' Thick legs projected from brief, ragged shorts. Beefy tattooed arms. His sloppy kiss. 'Real scorcher today, ain't it?

'Indeed.' An overwhelming odour of sweat and tobacco.

He slurped a can of beer. 'Have a good trip, babe?'

'Not… Not bad. I…I…have some gifts. Hope you like cigars, Fred.'

The pretty cardigan chosen for Kitty was large. But no matter how Kitty tried, the fronts refused to meet.

Mark and Alan ripped open their parcels. A cursory glance at their new shirts. They abandoned Forrester's expensive art books where they fell. Fell upon her afterthought: two packets of liquorice allsorts.

'Hey! Youse,' said Fred. 'Give over.'

The family devoured her sugary sweets. To think I feared the parents might worry about tooth damage, she thought.

Freddo brought home fish and chips for dinner. 'Let's celebrate your arrival, baby.'

A rare treat, it seemed, to sit around the table.

Freddo ripped open the white paper wrapping. 'Bog in, Auntie.'

Not a plate or utensil in sight. White bread with margarine. The boys tore flesh from the fish. Teeth chumped. In a trice, the meal was reduced to a few overcooked fragments of chips, backbone and ribs. The lads wiped greasy faces and hands on the paper.

Anna barely touched the food. 'I'll use your bathroom, if I may.'

Kitty led the way. 'An outdoor loo, auntie.' A concrete laundry tub sufficed for ablutions. 'Top and tail in the morning, dear.'

Anna lay in her lumpy bed. Hot. Not a bad breeze from the creaking fan. What was it they said about small blessings?

One day down. Nine to go.

In the morning, Kitty waved towards the rusting refrigerator. 'Help yourself, auntie.' Adding with pride, 'We're laid-back around here.'

A household without set meals? Anna blinked. The refrigerator contained cans of ale. Bread and jam, and a block of rat-trap cheese.

She scoured a plate. Ate a cheese sandwich. Tackled the grimy kitchen. Took up a broom. A miracle this place isn't overrun with mice, she thought.

Kitty's brow creased. 'Jeeze, auntie, why bother? It'll be just as bad tomorrow.'

Anna was shocked by the boys' bedtime: anywhere from nine to midnight.

Late one evening, she noticed illumination in their room. 'Shall I switch off the light?'

Kitty barely took her eyes from her *True Romance*. 'If you like.'

Piles of discarded jeans and T-shirts came as no surprise.

'But…you're in your day clothes?'

Mark shrugged. 'What's new?'

The boys appeared mid-morning. Made themselves jam or cheese sandwiches. Rushed out to play. Now and then, they attended school.

Freddo coughed and smoked. Disappeared for work. Anna never did discover his occupation.

Kitty asked to borrow fifty dollars. 'Until Freddo gets paid.'

The third time since I've been here, Anna thought, silently handing over the money. I'm unlikely to see a cent of it again. No matter. I've my return ticket, and cash to spare. To think she'd wasted so many years feeling inferior.

Anna coughed and sneezed. Emerged from her bed only for food or the loo. Took cold sponge baths. Yearning for a shower. Made herself toast with cheese and tea. Scalding the utensils prior to use. She crossed off every day of her calendar. Only three to go. Her horoscope foretold a sudden resolution. Time for a change.

The day before Anna was due to leave. Kitty barged into her room. 'Get ready, auntie. We're off to the shops.'

'If you don't mind, I'll stay here.' Anna still had a tickly throat.

Kitty stood, stolid and unmoving. 'Exercise will make you feel better, auntie.'

Head spinning, Anna dressed. Nothing will make me feel well until I've left this hovel, she thought. A trek in the blazing sun? The last thing I need.

Curious glances followed their progress down the street.

'I'm going to make a dress, auntie,' Kitty said. 'Can't find one in my size. The material costs about fifteen dollars a yard.'

Anna shrugged. 'Everything's dear these days. I need cough mixture.' She stepped into a pharmacy.

Kitty waited outside. 'Come to the material shop, auntie.'

Anna's niece chose a lurid floral.

'Five metres of fabric, thread and a zipper.'

The salesman said, 'That'll be eighty dollars.'

Anna paid. It's the least I can do, she thought.

Next stop, the toy shop. The boys grabbed a blue truck. Alan rummaged among paints.

Kitty giggled. 'Get whatever colours you like. How about some Lego?'

A red fire engine took Alan's eye.

An old-fashioned place. Anna sank into one of the chairs for weary customers. Amazed at her niece's shopping spree. It might be different if they ate proper food.

The shopkeeper grinned and rubbed his hands. 'So you hail from Honeysuckle Bay? Used to live in the city myself. Wouldn't go back, but.'

Anna faked a smile. Grateful for the ceiling fan. A few more hours…

The cash register clanged and clicked through a long list.

He beamed. 'The damage is one hundred and twenty-five dollars and ninety-five cents.'

But where was Kitty? And her boys?

The owner waited expectantly.

Anna extracted the notes from her purse.

'Your change.' The man pressed two twenties and a five-dollar bill into her sweating palm. 'Very generous, if I may say so. Poor kids.'

Kitty appeared. Grinning, she claimed her parcel.

Doesn't even have the grace to look guilty, Anna thought.

At first light, Anna dressed, already packed. Toast and tea. Farewell hugs. Barely ten minutes before her coach. Kitty looked bereft.

Freddo said, 'Do you have to leave, babe?'

Anna took off, afraid they meant her to stay. She gained the coach with seconds to spare.

Wait until I tell Forrester about his superior family. She chuckled. Tears rolled down her cheeks. Curious glances from other passengers.

The man across the aisle had a lovely smile. Nice eyes, too. 'Must be a good one. Do tell.'

'You wouldn't believe…'

'Try me.'

He indicated the empty seat beside her. 'Do you mind?'

'Not at all.'

Rob was a widower. Vulnerable. Lonely. It all poured out. Anna shared things she had never told anyone. It felt as if they had been friends for ever. They lunched and laughed in a café in some anonymous little town.

Laughed some more. Anna had words with the driver. She hardly noticed when she passed Honeysuckle Bay. Rob squeezed her hand. A gamble, she thought. But isn't that what life's all about?

Missing Reader

I shiver in January's brilliant sunshine. My very first day of school. Mum holds up her Box Brownie, captures the moment. In the long shadows of morning, Victor's face solemn. A smart trilby, brown and fawn striped jumper, shorts. A fat puppy at his feet. It had licked and jumped until he pinioned it between his heels.

My sister Curly gives a half-smile. She's cute in her blue, crocheted lace dress, a present from Nan. Everyone remarks on her mop of crinkled blonde hair.

Mine is straight as a pin, and no thicker since Mum cut it like that of a boy. But it has grown enough to sport a red bow. My face is partially shadowed, arms rigid at my sides. Mum had knitted my long green cardigan, and made the skirt. It looks very short on long legs.

The bus delivers mail and parcels. Not usually kids.

Mum leans towards the driver. 'Put them off at Belltrees School.' She says, 'Make sure you eat your lunch.'

A final kiss. Victor seems embarrassed.

'Wait until the bus stops before you get off. Make sure Dessie is with you.'

We're the sole passengers. I guess other children live close by. Mum holds Curley's hand, waving as the vehicle rumbles away.

Victor sits stiffly. Is he afraid of missing our stop? Or worried over Dad's stories of teachers who cane without mercy? Lessons on self-defence may have made him nervous, too.

The bus groans to a halt. We rush to alight. Victor whistles like Dad does, to keep his spirits up.

A cream weatherboard school meets my eager eyes. I've anticipated this moment for months.

A group of students stare at us.

Giggles from a pert blonde with neat plaits, smart uniform, shiny shoes. 'What a funny cardigan.'

'And look at her skirt, Jenny. Home-made, poor thing.'

Only then do I notice the skew-whiff red, blue and green checks across the front of my skirt. And I can guess why Aunt Linda, referring to Mum's knitting, had muttered about good wool spoilt.

The teacher doesn't offer buddies for the day. Or show us the toilets. We learn the teacher's name later. Mr Kurt.

In the classroom, he begins handing out brightly illustrated ABC and reading books. My shining moment of ownership is almost within reach.

'May I help, Mr Kurt?'

'Why, thank you, Jenny.' She takes over book distribution.

I picture one of the reading books in my hands. That silky cover, the sweet, new aroma…

Jenny places a reading book in front of each child.

Then the music stops. Right at the desk before mine. I blink back tears: their supply has run out.

Mr Kurt shrugs. 'You'll get yours when the stationery order arrives.'

We are meant to share. But every time I go to touch the book, my neighbour snatches it away. 'Mine.'

At recess, girls chatter and shriek. Nobody speaks to me. And I lack the courage to approach them. I have a major problem: location of the toilet. Mum says it isn't nice to discuss such matters. I decide to wait until we go home. It becomes difficult to hold out. I manage through the morning classes. By then, it's urgent.

Mr Kurt looms over me. 'Little girl…the new one. What's your name?

'Dessie Wright.'

'Didn't you hear me ask you a question?'

'No.'

'No, what?'

The class giggles. I flush, puzzled what he means.

'You must respond "Yes, sir" or "No, sir" to me. I asked about your religion. Victor, can you tell me?'

My brother shifts uneasily. 'Please, sir, what was the question?'

Mr Kurt rolls his eyes. 'Are you deaf, boy?'

'No, sir.'

'Jenny, perhaps you might enlighten this...'

'Fool?' offers someone.

Chuckles.

'Certainly, sir.' Her glance is triumphant. 'Which church do you attend?'

Victor's face flames. 'We don't go to church, sir.'

Glances of astonishment. Giggles.

'Where were you christened?'

'We weren't.'

In the shocked stillness, eyes swivel in our direction.

Daddy said we were fortunate to be freed from the fetters of religion. Whatever that meant. But it seems to me that Victor's words have confirmed suspicions: we are odd.

Lunch recess. I'm in agony.

Nearby, two girls spin a rope, feet skip. They count with growing excitement. Applesauce, mustard, spider. One, two, three, four...

Boys play cricket. They thwack balls against bats. Victor stands on the sidelines. A pariah like me.

I feel nauseous. Can't manage my sandwich. Luckily, Victor is occupied with his own concerns. He doesn't notice me throw it into a bin. I kneel in the playground. A posture of submission. The floodgates open.

Relief. Horror. Humiliation.

A damp and uncomfortable afternoon. I ignore whispers, and smothered titters. At long last, we go to catch the bus home.

Victor glares. 'You stink. That was the dumbest...'

'Didn't know where to find the toilet.'

'Couldn't you see those two small buildings on the hillside?'

Mum meets us at the door Victor drops his case on the floor. 'Dessie wet her pants. And I couldn't do my sums.'

Her brow creases. 'For goodness sakes…didn't Mr Kurt show you the toilets?'

'No. And I'm the only one in first class without a reader.'

'He didn't he give you one? And what happened about your arithmetic, Victor?'

'Other kids learnt long division last term.'

'Did they indeed?' She squeezes my arm. 'We'll soon sort this out.'

She pours hot water into a dish, brings a towel, washer, soap. It feels wonderful to be clean and in fresh clothes.

We enjoy a snack.

'Dessie, no doubt, your reading book will be there next week. I'll help you until then.' She talks Victor through his sums.

He grins. 'Thanks, Mum. They aren't hard, after all.'

Our second day of school. I won't make the same mistake again. But in one of the small buildings on the hill, I puzzle over a metal trough.

I join the others.

Children fall about with mirth. 'She goes to the boys' toilet.'

In class, Mr Kurt raps a ruler across my knuckles. 'I said to take out your reading book.'

'Please, sir…' Trembling. 'I don't have one.'

The class titters.

Mr Kurt brushes back strands of grey hair. 'Oh! You'll get yours later.'

We troop in from school. Mum asks, 'What did you learn today?'

'Nothing.'

'Did Mr Kurt give you a reader?'

'No, Mum.'

She purses her lips. 'I see.' Helps me with reading. Sets Victor a few sums.

Mr Kurt's game is played out weekly for six months.

Did Kurt make judgements based on middle-class values? Assuming that education would be wasted on the children of a rabbit-trapper, Dad's task back then? I know my parents felt angry with him. Doubtless at a loss how to tackle the situation.

I'll be forever grateful to have had a mother with the good sense and the ability to fill in his deficits until a return to the comprehensive lessons from Blackfriars Correspondence School.

The Infinite Mystery of Being

The albino unfurled his silken thread. A spaceman on his lifeline, he dreamt of exotic lands. A place where being white wouldn't matter.

He floated on air currents with legs outstretched. Spun until he felt giddy. Took the opposite direction. The feeling was terrific.

'Herbert Lester Spider, stop those silly games,' shouted Mother. 'You may be pale but at least you could try to be like your brothers. They've already learnt to weave a web.'

Herbert said, 'Sorry.' But he wasn't.

'One day, you'll venture too far and get dusted. Mrs Wapping loathes spiders.'

He gathered the gossamer onto his inner spool, furled it wide. Climbed up the thread, adjusting it with his claws. Climbed down. Lost track of time. Outside of time. Part of all time. Transfixed by the infinite mystery of being.

The moon cast a mellow light through the billowing lace curtains.

He thought, my thread is not only strong but pliable. It connected him to the windowsill. Drifting in his secret world, he pulsed with excitement. There was more to life than finding food. Why couldn't his mother understand?

The little fellow hurtled forth on his tiny cable. More skilful every day, he swung past Mrs Wapping's thick spectacles. The old dear couldn't see very well. And, luckily, never used those terrible gases. Legend had it, they had wrought havoc to his family when her husband was alive.

One minute, Herbert revelled in another sortie on his cable. The next, he became visible even to Mrs W. Illuminated in a ray of sunlight.

Her huge eyes peered through thick lenses. 'Dear, oh, dear. Jolly spiders.' A trembling hand grabbed the damp duster. It wiped a smeary path across the dusty windowsill. Destroying the family food web, along with cocooned offerings, ready for supper.

Herbert crouched in the shadows. His heart raced. Once, twice, Mrs Wapping struck out. He'd never know how he managed to escape.

Mother dropped down beside him. 'You idiot. Look what you've done. Took me weeks to build that web. Thanks to you, we'll all go hungry tonight.'

'Sorry. I didn't mean…'

'Sorry? I've heard that before. This silly cavorting around has to stop. It's time to learn the things spiders must know. Building a web, finding a mate. Later, of course, you'll get eaten like your father and elder brothers.'

'Eaten?' His eyes widened in horror. Several of his brothers had vanished. He had been grateful: free of their merciless teasing. Never for a moment had he imagined…

'Wives in this family eat their mates.'

'Not me. I want to live, see things.'

'Cats' whiskers. Your destiny is to catch flies and insects. Procreate, then die. You may look different to the others. But at least try to act like one of the family.'

'Honest, hardworking, sensible': he'd often heard it before. But eaten? There has to be some mistake. My quest has barely begun, a search within and beyond. His burning desire to voyage and discover could never be assuaged by food.

'The world doesn't end in the garden,' he faltered.

'Huh. It's the world now, is it? A foolish dreamer. Just like your father, Dog rest his soul.' Her voice was icy. 'You're clearly incapable of finding yourself a mate. I shall speak to Esmeralda. A matter of the greatest delicacy.'

Esmeralda? If Herbert Lester hadn't been albino, he would've turned white. Nothing about Esmeralda was delicate. Gross and hairy, her enormous web sagged with the spoils of victory. The ugly creature lived in a far corner of the room. He'd seen her greedily consuming something. Flies? Herbert had thought so at the time.

Mother took his silence as acquiescence. 'Good. I'm glad to see you're being sensible about this. I shall make the necessary arrangements.'

He pondered the best way to handle this development. Tonight might be his last chance to escape. A thin sliver of moon shone among the brilliant stars. Distracted, he barely noticed his younger brothers.

They chattered nearby. 'Where's the freak? What's old Whitey up to now?'

'Sulking, I expect,' said Mother.

They laughed.

'You all work so hard it isn't fair for Herbert to be treated differently. Helping himself to food we've caught.'

In the first pale light of dawn, Herbert Lester Spider set off. Fear jostled with excitement. He crept out through the open window. Fixed his silken thread to the sill. Floated down, down, down. Into the great unknown world.

Touchdown. A vast grey land stretched far into the distance. It felt cold and unyielding beneath each of his hairy tarsus. His legs picked up changes in the air and delicious new aromas.

Beyond was something Mother called a tree. He recalled her saying it provided shelter for outdoor spiders. A wonderful place to find food.

Away from jibes and criticism, Herbert savoured his freedom. Enjoying the hushed and expectant stillness before birds tweeted their first songs. He must be far from the house before the glow of pink, gave way to heat and danger. The world awaited.

He scurried on and on. His legs slowed under a brassy sky. Hot and sticky, he wondered. Will he ever reach the sanctuary of that tree? Fearing the swish of wings. A sharp beak.

At last cool shadows. Bliss.

Herbert ascended the trunk. Weary now, he fixed his silken thread to a limb. Swayed back and forth in the breeze. Eyed the splendour of grass and scented flowers far below.

He was ravenous. Herbert pushed aside hunger and thirst. He hadn't appreciated how hard it might be to survive on his own. But anything was better than life…and death…with Esmerelda.

The little fellow tried a few tentative acrobatics. His stomach growled so badly he couldn't concentrate. If only he knew how to construct a web, it would be easy. He tried, but couldn't fathom where to begin. Got himself into a frightful muddle.

He pounced on a tiny fly. A brief struggle and he sucked energy into his exhausted body. A little spasm of pleasure. He wiped the residue from his face. 'That's better.'

He sensed, rather than saw, the sharp eyes and even sharper beak. Rushed for the nearest knot hole.

'Hey, where do you think you're goin'?'

'S-sorry, sir.' Herbert scuttled along the branch, abseiled to another, found a small alcove. Good: well-hidden by leaves, and no prior tenant. He curled up inside and fell asleep. Dreamt of days gone by and never known.

The flitter of wings. Herbert woke in an instant, expecting attack. Not a bird but a splendid butterfly fluttered on a branch. Wings patterned in blues and yellows of every hue. Dots of pure gold, circled black.

These creatures are usually the prey of spiders, he thought. But this one glows with the force of a different destiny. Never had he seen such luminous eyes.

'Sorry to scare you.' Her voice seemed pure music. 'I've been expecting you, Herbert Lester Spider.

'How do you know my name?'

'I'm here to help you find great truths in far-off lands.'

He gulped. 'Are there dangers?'

'Nothing is ever achieved without risk. You'll learn in your own way.'

'Perhaps I ought to…'

'See your family again?'

'Before I go. Let them know I'm all right.' He pictured Esmerelda. 'Maybe not.'

'They don't live there any more.'

'What?

'Last night, Mrs Wapping went to hospital. A stroke. Her niece cleaned the house. Dust and cobwebs flew.'

He didn't ask how she knew. Moisture sparkled in his eyes.

'Weep not, little one. You'll meet again in a different place. Another kind of time.'

'I've been a great disappointment.'

'Your mother planned to sacrifice you, remember. To be true to others, be true to yourself. Are you ready?'

He trembled 'Is…is it a long journey?'

'Short as the blink of an eye. Longer than forever. A day or a life is all the same to me.' She grabbed a brown leaf. 'Take this. Sling your gossamer around several times. Firmly attach it.'

Herbert spun his web, fixing the tiny basket. Climbed inside. Anchored a seat belt.

The butterfly cried, 'Ready?'

Herbert Lester Spider quivered. 'Suppose birds attack us?'

'We're invisible to harmful creatures. Take-off!' The butterfly soared. Not fluttering, but speeding. Faster and faster.

Houses and gardens dropped away. Land and oceans merged, green with blue. Our travellers vanished among the galaxies of stars.

A Dangerously Rusty Ladder

Jamie's wail cut through her sleep like an electric knife. Dessie was out of bed before her muscles could respond. Staggering. Caught between a pleasant dream and the demands of young Jamie.

In the darkness, she pushed on her slippers. This is the fourth time I've been up tonight. Neville hadn't stirred. Not once. Men. Dessie felt ready to drop.

She snapped on the nursery light. Jamie clung to the side of the cot. Normally the sight of his blond curls was irresistible. But at three a.m.?

Tears rolled down his chubby cheeks. His face broke into a grin. 'Mumma.'

'Lie down, Jamie.' Her voice carried the sharp edge of irritation. She loved him so deeply. But nobody had warned her that motherhood would be so darned hard. She envied her unmarried friends sleeping through the whole night. Or out having fun. While I'm trapped here, at the beck and call of a two-year-old.

Dessie glimpsed herself in the mirror. Dark shadows under the eyes, blonde hair overdue for a trim. I look a frump, she thought. Could be thirty instead of twenty-two.

Her friend Sylvie had remained childless. By choice. Maybe she was right? Dessie's heart softened. She thought of everything that was lovable about Jamie. The giggles and hugs. His precious first words. The tentative steps, his face aglow with the joy of achievement.

Dessie picked him up. Relished the warm firmness of his sturdy little body. She'd be devastated if anything happened to him. Maybe his nappy was wet? Woken by discomfort. No, not that. She touched his forehead: no fever.

Jamie giggled, pleased at this new game.

She gave him a drink and put him down. Firm now. 'Go to sleep, son.'

Jamie's eyes filled with anguish. 'Mumma. Stay boy.'

'Go to sleep.' She tucked in the sheets. Patting the restless child until he drifted off.

Dessie crawled back into bed. Chilled all over, she turned the electric blanket to high. If Jamie cried again, Neville would just have to go. He had been the one in a rush to start a family. Encouraging her to be a full-time mother, rather than put Jamie into day care. She had concurred in his decision.

Dessie lay awake for ages. Afraid to move into a more comfortable position, lest she disturbed Neville. Dessie had read somewhere that the first six months of a baby's life were the most difficult. She had clung to the thought during night feeds and insoluble tears.

The miracle must happen soon.

Somewhere, an alarm clock wailed. Dessie drifted, trapped at the bottom of a high cliff. There was a dangerously rusty ladder, loose in its moorings. Steps were missing. In a panic, she searched for escape. Knowing there was none.

Neville touched her on the shoulder. 'How'd you sleep, sweetie?'

'I was up to Jamie four times.'

He sighed. 'I know it isn't easy for you. But I work, while you can rest during the day.'

'Yeah, sure.' He just didn't get it. An active toddler seldom let a mother take a break.

Jake threw back the bedclothes. Opened a drawer. Set out a row of odd socks on the quilt. 'How do you lose so many? Where do they go?'

'One of life's great mysteries,' Dessie snapped. After such a night, nothing was less appealing than talk of missing socks. It implied carelessness on her part.

The bedside radio played 'Talking, talking, Happy talk. If you don't have a dream, how you gonna make a dream come true?'

Neville scrabbled through his drawer. 'Where are my blue socks to match this suit?'

'Oh, let me.' She flung the missing items onto the bed. 'Next time, look under things.'

'Where are my car keys?' Neville searched his pockets. 'Make me a coffee, sweetie. And perhaps an egg.'

She flounced into the kitchen. The toaster rejected the slice of bread. Yawning, she gave the appliance a shake. Voila. Dessie cracked a couple of eggs into the pan. She thought, if only it were me rushing off to an important meeting.

An acrid smell of burnt toast assailed her nostrils. She dropped the spoilt slices into the bin. Turned on the exhaust fan.

Neville popped his head around the door. 'Something burning?'

'Burnt. We need a new toaster.'

'I'll just have bread then.'

After breakfast, Neville emerged from the nursery with a wide grin. 'Jamie looks so cute. Come and look.'

'Please. Let him sleep. I need a while…on my own.'

He looked surprised. 'But I thought…'

She sighed. 'Give me a break. I saw too much of Jamie last night.'

He shrugged. Gave her a quick peck on the cheek.

She lingered disconsolately over the dishes. Everyone pretended a baby brought a never-ending feast of excitement. The reality? No more spontaneous outings to the movies. No long lunches with colleagues from work. And, given the cost of babysitters, they were always the first to rush home from any party.

Jamie gurgled his way through cereal. Afterwards, Dessie sponged his face and hands. Wiped the high chair. Put him on his potty. He liked to sit there reading his book. Hopefully, he would soon be free of napkins. But she avoided making it an issue. The clinic sister said too many psychological problems resulted from obsessive toilet training.

With her son occupied, she rushed to the laundry. Put a load of nappies in the machine. Finished some hand-washing. Meant to return immediately to supervise her son. But stood, transfixed. A woman spoke on the radio about her latest overseas trip.

Once, shortly after their marriage, they'd booked a passage to Europe. At the urging of Neville's father, they'd cancelled. Using their joint savings as a deposit on their house. We could have travelled and had a family later, Dessie thought. My dreams shattered. She still felt cheated.

Dessie heard crashes and bangs from next door. What on earth were her neighbours doing? The sounds included breaking glass. It took seconds to realise that the noises came from her own house. Oops, I forget to take Jamie from his potty. She sprinted for the kitchen.

Jamie sat among saucepans and dishes. He banged away with a meat tenderiser. Her eyes bulged: her Swedish jug and glasses reduced to shards of broken glass. He must have dragged that chair to the cupboard. Fetching her treasures down from the top shelf.

His huge grin. 'Mumma.'

It defied reason, but no other explanation presented itself.

'Sit still, son.' Praying that he stayed unmoving, Dessie crept closer. Scarcely daring to breathe. She leant down and scooped him up. Berating herself for being so careless. Miraculously, he had only sustained one tiny scratch. She trembled with shock and relief.

'Mumma.' His chuckles morphed into a pucker of anxiety at her worried expression. His white jumpsuit was covered with tiny slivers of glass.

She put his contaminated clothing into the bin. Bathed and dried him. Put on his gown. Dumped him in the cot.

He yelled, 'No, no. Boy walk.'

Dessie felt close to tears. 'I know you hate being in your crib at this hour. But Mummy has your big mess to clean up.'

The child sobbed.

My sister's beautiful wedding present, she thought, Never got to use them. Not once. Anger gave way to guilt. I shouldn't have left the child alone for so long. Kids get into danger so quickly.

The house felt like a prison.

Dessie said, 'Let's go out for a while. It'll make us both feel better.'

She brought out the stroller. Jamie's tears changed to giggles. He kicked his navy shoes against the footrest.

At the shopping-centre, strangers smiled and chucked him under the chin. 'He's so cute in those jeans and yellow top.'

Dessie forced a smile. It's easy enjoying babies and young children, without the responsibility of raising them. She window-shopped. Greeting people she knew.

'Goodness. Jamie isn't a baby any more.' Molly Barden was an acquaintance. Frizz of brown hair, warm smile. 'My word, he's a lovely little lad. But they grow up too quickly, don't they?'

Dessie swallowed. Jamie looks angelic, she thought. But you'd never guess his mischievous side. Or the depth of my frustration.

Something about Dessie's expression alerted Molly to the young mother's low mood. She stopped gushing. Tears shone in her blue eyes. 'But you wouldn't want him to remain a baby forever, would you?'

Over coffee, her soft voice told of the anguish and struggle to raise Terry, her hyperactive, autistic son. Sleepless nights with Jamie were nothing compared to Terry's behaviour issues. 'Temper tantrums, broken walls and furniture. We needed locks on every cupboard door, even the refrigerator.' She wiped her eyes. 'Two of my children were in high school. My elder son was studying for the HSC. Nobody slept. Terry could scale a six-foot fence. Impossible to control. Once, he went missing.'

'Oh, dear. How long before…'

'Two whole days. The police brought him back, scratched and dirty. We never discovered where he'd been. Finally, we had to…to…'

Dessie could barely trust herself to speak. 'Find a care home?'

Molly nodded. 'The doctor told me I was on the verge of a breakdown. I had my health, three other children and my husband to consider…' She trembled. 'Made the hardest decision of my life.'

'But you had no choice. How old…?'

'Fifteen when he was admitted.'

Dessie felt ashamed of her lack of patience with Jamie. 'Incredible you managed so long.'

'A lot of people say that. Terry couldn't speak, yet he knew we were family. Ran eagerly to greet us. His accusing eyes when we left broke my heart.' She blotted her eyes. 'Didn't know until much later that he scarcely ate during the first week. He cried every time I went home.'

'Poor you,' said Dessie, a catch in her voice. 'Did he settle?'

'Oh, Terry's happy these days. After a visit, he looks forward to going back. Took me a long time to accept my decision, though. Inside, I never will. It's unbearable, knowing that your child will always remain dependant. You must thank God for your healthy son.'

'Oh, I do. I really do.'

They hugged.

'Your story helps to put everything into perspective. And I hope it will make me a better mother.'

The Specimen

She stepped aboard the train. Tall and stately, eyes cool and intelligent.

A youngish man observed her with more than casual interest. In her fifties, he guessed. Lunching in town, perhaps?

Grey silk blouse, burnished with silver. Glitter buttons. Long silver earrings, a necklet band of silver clasped at the front of her throat, in a style known as 'the kiss'. Oatmeal slacks, a patterned grey and pinkish silk velvet scarf.

He never left home without his sketch pad. This exotic specimen would enhance his collection. Perhaps it was his imagination, but he sensed a rapport between them.

He craved to start sketching. But there were all sorts of restrictions on art these days. Invasion of privacy, all that. Almost every freedom of expression had been eroded. Cameras banned, even at the local sports carnival. One was afraid to risk prosecution, however innocent the intent.

Should he seek her permission?

She slid into a seat opposite. Her head resting against the corner seat. Eyes closed. Perhaps she was tired after a sleepless night. Maybe fighting a viral infection?

An ephemeral moment. A fragile butterfly of time to be seized before it vanished. With rising excitement, he flicked the pages of his notebook, past annotations and quick sketches. Found a virgin surface.

He took out a 2B pencil, steadied the quiver in his hand. Those first, sure strokes pleased him. He captured that noble profile, the folds of scarf, the curve of her eyes under the lids.

The woman stirred at each station, glancing through the window. Afraid of missing her stop? Like a guilty schoolboy, he hid his work.

Once, her glance skimmed over the pad. A glint of amusement in her eyes. He felt certain she had guessed what he was doing. Held his breath. A co-conspirator, she pretended not to notice.

He took several furtive glances. Adding here, cross-hatching there. Shortly before she rose to leave, he made the final stroke. Sighed with satisfaction. Dying to return to his studio and take up the brushes. The image he had created must remain a mystery to her. Unless she happened upon the finished painting in some gallery.

A Walk In Darkness

Kings Cross. The most cosmopolitan place in Sydney. It glittered with risqué excitement. Lynda Blake recalled dreamy evenings in the fifties, dancing at the Tabou with her latest date to 'That Old Black Magic' or 'Fever'. Lingering afterwards over cappuccinos. Lured by the spicy aroma of little coffee shop in the small hours. Driving home in old bombs, now collector's items, worth a fortune.

How strange to return like this, she thought. Her smiling image was reflected in a shop window: shortish grey hair, green eyes. Young-looking for her age. If it hadn't been for that darned aching back…

Lynda had quailed at the doctor's prognosis. 'These things get worse with age. You'll be in a wheelchair by the time you're thirty.'

She avoided his powerful drugs. They did more harm than good over the long term. His dire predictions didn't eventuate. Lately, though, depression cloaked her waking hours. Desperate for pain relief, if not a cure.

A friend suggested a healer in the Cross. Lynda made an appointment. What had she to lose? The possibility of improvement brought a glimmer of hope, long absent.

Harold knew nothing of the excursion. Her husband would have dismissed the idea as quackery. The pleasure brought by a simple outing was ridiculous. The cityscape rushed past the train window.

Her husband had declared they couldn't afford a second car, so she had never learnt to drive. Her world shrank to the size of a suburban cottage and the local shopping centre. It had happened so gradually, she was barely aware of it – until now.

Lynda walked down Darlinghurst Road. Lurid shops had proliferated since her youth. Closed in the innocence of morning. Few tourists were about. She pictured them lingering over late breakfasts in their hotels. Gathering strength for that daily jaunt of doing Sydney.

She had nervously suggested updating her office skills.

Harold wouldn't hear of it. 'I don't want a wife of mine working. You can't combine household duties with a career. You'd do neither job well.' He patted her shoulder. 'Mother always said how nice it is for a woman to take pride in her home.'

Pride? Her mother-in-law invariably carried a duster, can of furniture polish and rag around the house. Wiped rings from under glasses, even while guests were drinking. Adjusted cushions every time anyone breathed. Plucked imaginary lint from the patterned rug.

Lynda gritted her teeth. She found one way to ease her frustrations. Banging the iron down hard on Harold's shirts. Crashing it back into the metal holder. She smoothed out wrinkles with her hands, before the next onslaught. Watching her husband sink lower and lower behind his paper. It brought her such glee.

Lynda strolled on. She gazed into the windows of little boutiques. Lovely clothes and high prices. With Harold's modest income, she could never afford to buy any of them. If only I were working, she thought, we could buy nice things. Go out more. She adored the theatre. They hadn't seen a show in ages.

She recalled the girls' schooldays. Lunches to pack. Uniforms to keep spotless. Speech and play nights. Now her daughters were married. One in Queensland and the other overseas. She spent the greater part of her days alone, longing to put her life back on track. Not quite sure how to work such a miracle.

Harold grumbled if she invited guests. These days, he snoozed in front of the TV. She craved the joy of a real conversation. Anything to make her feel alive, rather than existing. Trapped in this no-woman's-land between youth and old age.

One evening, she had switched off the set. Shouting at him, 'Is this all there is? What life's all about?'

Harold blinked behind his bifocals. 'I…uh…must have fallen asleep,' he said. Wondering if this outburst resulted from the Change. Chaps at work spoke about it. 'The film, you mean? Oh, it was about the war…'

'No. No.' She stamped her foot. 'I wasn't talking about the jolly TV. I meant us.'

'Not feeling well, dear?'

Tears stung her eyes. 'Life seems so pointless.'

'Just sit down, luv. I'll rustle up a cuppa.'

'I don't want tea… Oh, forget it.'

She stormed out, slamming the door. Tears mingled with the soapsuds of a bubble bath. She reclined in the warm water. Can I continue in this marriage?

The Fitzroy Gardens brought a schizophrenic mix of palms, tree-ferns, tropical plants and English trees. A haven for hungry pigeons which accosted new arrivals. Lynda saw an elderly man in a threadbare navy suit on one of the seats. He rubbed his hands against the chill breeze. Guarding his position in a pool of sunlight.

Lynda felt impervious to the cold. She stopped to admire the El Alamein Fountain. Elegant as the gossamer parachutes of dandelions she had blown into the wind as a child. The cool mist caressed her face. She trembled with delight.

It was too early for her appointment. She sat down on one of the benches. Noticed a young girl nearby, in a motley layering of shabby clothing. A street kid, she supposed. The teenager held a ragged piece of rope which served as a leash for her scruffy, half-grown Labrador. The big pup wore a silly grin. It jumped around, excitedly wagging his tail.

The girl balanced a milkshake, while controlling an exuberant animal. His rope leash became entangled. The cardboard container dropped. Spilling the contents. A stunned silence.

The girl wailed, 'Oh, shit. Why does it always happen to me?' She burst into noisy sobs.

Her pup hungrily lapped up the milk.

Lynda had seldom seen such anguish on a young face. I've only a few dollars, she thought, but must do something. She extracted a five-dollar note. Pressed it into the girl's hand. 'Please. Have this. Buy yourself another drink. I'm sorry it's not more.'

'No, it's all right,' sniffed the girl.

'I insist. Do the same for someone else when you can.'

Lynda walked away, a lump in her throat. What a sad time to be young. Jobs hard to find. Struggling to maintain self-respect, surviving on the dole. It was awful to think of youngsters in squats. Washing in cold water, lacking electricity. Doing whatever was necessary in order to eat.

Her generation had lived with the spectre of the Bomb. But in the days after the Second World War, employment was easy to find. Teenagers looked forward to a bright future. Now adolescents were cynical about their prospects.

She entered the council-run toilet block. It smelt of antiseptic. Crude, drug-related graffiti adorned the walls. Drying her hands, she noticed a woman of indeterminate age sprawled like an abandoned doll on a bench. Drugs, drink or simply a place to sleep? Lynda hurried away. Feeling almost guilty at having invaded the woman's privacy.

Lynda lingered at a jewellery shop. Intricate gold bracelets, diamonds, sapphires... Pondering the gap between this luxury and those folk glimpsed in the last hour.

'Excusa me,' said a voice. 'I'm a stranger here. From Melbourne. Could you tell me the way to Bondi, please?'

She glanced up. Took in his Italian shoes, the expensive suit. He was handsome in a mature way with warm brown eyes and darkish eyes.

'Bondi?' She struggled to give sensible directions. Oddly discomforted under his amused glance. Glad she had dressed for the occasion. A slim-fitting check woollen skirt and maroon blouse set off her figure to perfection.

'Isn't it a bit cool for the beach?' She laughed, feeling alive for the first time in years.

He shrugged. 'Maybe you're right. Say, how about joining me for a drink?'

She felt a rush of excitement. It was years since a man had tried to pick her up. 'Oh, no, I… I don't think so.'

He had a winning smile. 'Why not? Just a little drink?'

'I don't even know you.'

'Oh, scusi. Angelo Baretti. Forty-six years old, quite…'ow you say, armless?'

'Harmless?' She giggled. Savouring the hint of danger. Longing to accept.

His hand touched her sleeve. Burning to the flesh. 'Well, what do you say?'

She heard herself saying recklessly. 'Well, why not?' Suddenly, she noticed the time. 'Gosh. I have an appointment in a few minutes.'

'Meet me afterwards. Say in an hour?'

'But…where?'

'How about the fountain?'

She nodded, watching him stroll away. Lord…I'm behaving like a foolish teenager. Why didn't I say goodbye?

A drab building in a side street. Lynda glanced uneasily along the gloomy corridor. Stepped into an ancient lift, acrid with old oil. It creaked to the second floor. Her friend had been a patient here, so it must be OK.

She knocked on the healer's apartment door. Tall with dark, piercing eyes, he motioned her inside. The treatment room pulsated with New Age music. Books on meditation and healing. Noted an impressive array of metaphysical diplomas ranged along one wall.

He said, 'I can guarantee nothing. Sometimes the treatment works dramatically after only one session. Often, it takes much longer. Maybe it won't work at all…I can't tell. I don't actually touch you. My hands move a few inches from your body.' His voice sounded oddly comforting.

Lynda sat on an elegant straight-backed chair. Closed her eyes. Music eddied and swirled around her. His hands hovered near her body, moved above her head. She felt a peculiar sensation of warmth. Suddenly, she blinked back to full awareness.

The healer told her, 'Until next week.'

Lynda walked outside. The pain seemed less disturbing. Or was it her imagination?

She felt euphoric. Startled by the clarity and harshness of midday light. Excited at the prospect of meeting Angelo. Longing to savour for a little while the joy of being alive. Irritated with herself, too. Why not disappear into the tiled newness of Kings Cross station and go home?

She had warned her girls against this very situation.

'Hi, there.'

She looked around. 'Oh, hello.'

Now his smile seemed just a shade too wide and assured.

'I know a bar,' he said, smooth as an olive. 'They serve a very nice cocktail.'

She heard the clang of a warning bell. Where had she read the advice, never play the other man's game? 'I don't drink alcohol in the morning,' she said. 'I'd prefer a coffee.'

'Just one little drink? What harm…'

'No… No, really. I just want some coffee.'

She felt conspicuous walking beside the stranger. Surely passers-by must guess the circumstances of their meeting? She chose a cosy little restaurant with discreet lighting.

It seemed Angelo's marriage had broken down. He didn't believe in divorce. 'Don't want to marry again. Need a mature woman for dancing, outings. A good time.'

Lynda sipped her cappuccino. Nibbled her slice of Black Forest cake. Surprised that she couldn't stop thinking of Harold. Suddenly he seemed dear and dependable. Had his faults, certainly. But he was always there when she needed him. They'd been through so much together. It was worth addressing their problems. Maybe see a marriage counsellor?

'We could go somewhere after lunch,' Angelo was saying.

Lynda smiled. She toyed with her coffee. When her back improved, she'd insist on getting a job. It was the moment to take life into her own hands. Perhaps she could do something voluntary as well. Work with homeless kids? There were many people who needed help in these troubled times.

'So what do you think, about this afternoon?'

'I'd better not,' she said. 'My husband is very jealous.'

'But he need never know.'

She glanced at her watch. 'Actually, I'm expecting him soon.'

Angelo turned white. 'Here?' He glanced towards the window.

'Harold said he might come. Even now, he could be outside looking for me. I'd better go.'

'Yes, yes. Good idea.' He was on his feet, agitated. 'I wait here a little while.'

She opened her purse.

'No, no.' Angelo said. 'Don't worry. I pay.'

'How kind. Well, goodbye, Angelo. Nice meeting you.'

Lynda left. Outside she giggled at how keen Angelo had become to get rid of her. Tonight, she would make herself look especially attractive. Cook a fabulous meal. She went to catch her train.

Epiphany

Brilliant sunshine. Slim and lithe, Mum takes the lead. 'What a perfect day for our ramble.'

We barely notice one tiny cloud.

Druce holds her hand.

'Shh! Kids, look. Over there.'

A robin redbreast whistles. A delight of rising syllables and repetitions.

Whoosh of wings. Flash of red and blue. Whisper of eucalypt, turpentine and sassafras. Dappled by radiant light. Twisting vines, hairy tree ferns, purple fungi and rotting logs. A renaissance of moss. The peep of tiny red and purple fungi.

'Wow!' I said. 'Fairies' brollies.'

Mum nods. 'So they are. Look, Druce.'

My brother tried to grab one.

'No, darling, we mustn't spoil them.'

Vivi offer him two buttercups and a white violet instead.

Green fronds of ferns sway over my head. I love the soft, red fur near the base of each leaf. Almost the texture of human hair. New leaves curl up like snails. They fascinate me.

The fragrance of wild herbs and violets. Mum breathes the arcane green aroma. The sweet scent brings a sense of well-being, us in harmony with the forest.

'You'd never get air like this in town.'

Water gurgles over rocks. She carries Druce across. One of three streams, it joins others to form the head of the Hunter River.

She says that icy water seeps from natural springs. High on the hillside, moisture trickles through clefts in contours of the earth. I step carefully from one big stone to another, crossing the rippling stream. Vivi balances precariously. Her short legs barely make the next foothold. We scoop up water with our hands. The mossy flavour is the nicest I've ever tasted. I recall city visitors, amazed that it's safe to drink.

Mounds of sphagnum moss beg to be caressed.

Mum shakes her head. 'Keep right away. Funnel-web spiders lurk in nests underneath them.'

Lichen trails in palest green. It hangs from the limbs of tea trees, unkempt beards of old men. Others, sculptured like embossed wallpaper, cling to smooth trunks.

Willy-wagtails are dancing in the midday bright. And in a sudden hush, the one cloud is weeping. A glitter of raindrops. Translucent orbs of wonder, magnified, by some trick of the light. Huge glass balls drifting slowly, one by one. Rainbows in flight.

The amazing spectacle ends. Have I woken from a dream? Imagined the whole thing?

'I've never seen anything quite so lovely,' Mum whispers, 'and doubt I ever will again.'

Geographically Impossible

Way back in 1957, I unlocked the navy blue mailbag. Poured forth its treasure. Among the letters, I spied one for me. An unknown hand.

I ripped it open, and gasped. 'Gosh! My first twenty-first party invitation.' And probably my last, I thought, living fifty miles from Scone. In those days, they called it geographically impossible. Isolated farm. No transport.

I'd met the Wilkinses only once, friends of Auntie Violet. Surprise bubbled with delight. Imagine Mrs Wilkins thinking of me.

She enclosed a very nice letter for Mum. 'I promise to take good care of your daughter, should she be allowed to attend.'

Mum scowled. 'There's so much work to do here.'

Hopes juggled with disappointment. If only Auntie Aileen or cousin Polly were there. They'd put in a word on my behalf.

'Please, please, Mum. It'll be a chance for me to meet people of my age. It's only a weekend.'

'It's not fair that you should be the only one enjoying yourself.'

Jealous of her own seventeen-year-old daughter? My sister, Vivi, shot me a look.

Mum's cold note to Peter's mother made me cringe. 'Dessie may go, providing she is home on the Tuesday mail car.'

It made me feel like a stray parcel.

Vivi danced me around the bedroom. 'So they work in town. But home's on the Central Coast? I'm so pleased for you, sis.'

Then came the agony of what to wear.

Dad arrived home from town with a mysterious box. 'See what you think of this.'

My eyes widened. A strapless turquoise organza gown. Diamanté scattered over the draped bodice. I hugged him. 'Thank you, Daddy. I love it.'

Mum's face was a study of disapproval. 'Must have cost a fortune. And it's so bare. Be sure to wear the bolero.'

Daddy dropped me in town. Yippee! Three days of freedom.

The Wilkins clan brought a laugh a minute. It was a delight to be with such fun people. We drove off into the sunset. Passed rolling Central Coast beaches. Breathed in sea breezes. Pelicans floated by on lakes, every ripple painted red.

My eyes widened at the huge function room. Chandeliers. Thick carpet. I pictured myself descending that wide, curving staircase. Star from a Hollywood movie.

One of the girls helped zip up my gown. I ignored the bolero.

Mrs Wilkins stood back admiringly. 'Well, well, well. You look stunning.'

A blush warmed my cheeks. Others wore simple dresses. I guessed mine was way too formal. Thrilled by the glamour of my bare shoulders and décolleté.

We sang, 'For He's a Jolly Good Fellow'. Female relatives and friends kissed Peter. I gave him a peck on the cheek. He looked startled. Afterwards, he kept glancing my way. Doubtless, his mother saw the possibilities.

Surprise, surprise! Peter drove me back to the house. So different to Mum's negative attitude towards girls who attempted friendship with Victor.

On the way, Peter stopped his old jalopy. He made tentative conversation. I could see he felt shy. Squeezed his arm. He drew me closer. Finally, that kiss… Another…

Giggling, I told him of Mum's rule. 'Six months dating, before kissing a boy.'

He chuckled. 'That's a good one.' Peter adjusted his tie. Looked guilty. 'Guess we'd better join the party. Let's go round the back. So nobody will notice.'

I put a comb through my short hair. We crept into the kitchen – and right into the midst of friends and relatives. Everyone chuckled.

Peter's father roared with laughter. 'Aha! Sneaking in the back way.'

I winked. 'The car broke down.'

Mr Wilkins grinned. 'Told you we wouldn't be responsible after you arrived home.'

The merry bunch of partygoers came and went. Friends, aunties, uncles and cousins. Grandparents, sisters and brothers joined in the celebration. Oh the joy, the carefree atmosphere. Jokes, pop music and laughter took us into the early hours.

I fell asleep in a double bed between two of his aunts.

Sunday brought a golden autumn day. At Norah Head beach, every wave sparkled, under wide, cloudless skies. I breathed the briny tang. Given the cool breeze, Peter and I abandoned the idea of surfing.

'Let's build a sandcastle.' One pleasure I'd missed as a child.

Peter didn't hesitate. We giggled, adding turrets and a moat. Walked hand in hand, around the rocks. Took photographs of the lighthouse and each other. Every moment glowed.

That night, we played records. Everything from rock and roll to the classics and opera. All from his father's marvellous collection.

Finally, his mother shooed us off to our beds. 'I think it's time…' Gentle and caring. A world away from the angst I'd have endured at home.

Peter drove me back to Scone. We laughed at old jokes and new. Sang songs like '*Que Sera, Sera*', 'All I Have to Do is Dream' and the Everly brothers' 'Bye, Bye, Love'. How marvellous to be part of the teenage world.

I caught the mail truck home. Pop tunes, jokes and laughter spun around my head. Dreading my return to the gloom of our farm.

Mum and Victor's melancholy fell on me like a sack of potatoes. I felt like running away.

She moaned. 'We've all had terrible colds.'

Making me feel their illness was somehow my fault.

Adding, 'A lot of jobs weren't done while you were away. It's time to pull your weight.'

Vivi asked me about the party. The only one.

Desperate to salvage a few shreds of happiness, I shared one of Peter's jokes. A laugh would cheer them up. I faltered to the punchline. Stony faces.

Vivi and I shared an agonised glance.

Mum sniggered. 'Laugh, Victor, laugh. Wasn't that funny?

He said, 'I couldn't laugh and be a hypocrite. I'd split my face.'

Mum beamed. 'Of course you couldn't, son.'

I slammed into the bedroom. 'I'll never again share anything with that...'

'Miserable pair?' Vivi giggled. 'Ignore them. I'm so glad you had fun.'

I hugged her. 'Thanks for the support, sis. Makes all the difference.'

Another year before I made known my plans.

Vivi groaned. 'How will I manage without you?'

'It'll soon be your turn...'

Michael's Choice

I loathe the role of peace-maker, Marta thought, brushing back short grey hair. It isn't getting any easier. If only Tod would see reason.

Michael hadn't risen yet. No wonder, after his father's outrageous behaviour last evening.

Marta knocked on their son's door. 'Mike, darling. Can I fetch you a coffee?'

No response.

'Mike…'

With sudden foreboding, she peeped inside. Gasped. His bed was unslept in. Her hands shook. Perhaps Michael had spent the night with friends, Marta thought. Funny, I didn't hear him go out.

His car was gone from the garage. She dialled one number after another. Struggled to sound upbeat. Each call brought a negative response. Surely Karen would know his whereabouts? But she didn't have his girlfriend's number. I can't ring every Wong in the book, she thought.

She found the note later. Tucked under his pillow. It brought her little comfort. Wait until I show this to Tod, she thought.

The grandfather clock chimed. One p.m. 'Please call me, Michael,' Marta said to herself. 'Just call me.'

Two p.m. Nothing. She lifted the receiver. Put it down. I don't want to make a fool of myself. Darn it, she thought, he could be lying somewhere out there. Injured.

She dialled the police station. 'My…my son, Michael Dawson… he…he's left home. Missing, I mean. She felt silly. 'He's not slept in his bed…'

'Michael Dawson. Age of this lad?'

'Nineteen.'

She head a guffaw. 'Lady, if we chased every nineteen-year-old who did a bunk.'

'An argument…with his father…'

'Isn't it always?' A bored voice. 'Give him time to cool down. Call back in a week. If he's not back.' He hung up before she could tell him about the note.

Marta paced. Tod should be informed. She froze in the act of reaching for the phone. Her husband wouldn't welcome being disturbed for family matters. Not at the office.

At that moment, the device shrilled.

Marta rushed to pick it up. 'Michael?'

'Mrs Dawson?' A hesitant voice. 'I'm Karen Wong's mother. Like to speak with daughter, please.'

'Sorry… Karen isn't here.'

'Must be mistake. Last night Michael ring. He say Karen go to your place. Where my Karen?'

Marta went numb. 'Maybe she left with…'

'Mike? Where they go?'

'You tell me.'

'Oh, dear, dear… What to do?'

'They could be trying to telephone…'

'Yes, yes … You phone me, missus, when…'

'When I hear? Yes, of course. I need your contact details.' Marta scrawled the number.

At least he wasn't alone. That brought a measure of comfort. Karen was a lovely girl. If only Tod wasn't so…so negative about her. She daren't even think the word 'racist'.

She recalled his rant. 'That bloody Chinese has given you silly ideas.'

'I'll not stop seeing Karen,'

'While I'm paying, boyo, you'll do what I say.'

'Dad, you know that I've always wanted to paint.'

'I'll not have any son of mine mincing around some art school.'

'It's my life…'

'Don't rile me, boy. Decide on a university course. Medicine, law…
I'll back you to the hilt.'

'Art is a tertiary…'

'With no future in it. How many painters make money, tell me
that?'

In the drawing room, Marta sank into her chintz armchair. Stared
into the gathering dusk. Lights winked across the city. People hurried
home. Once, she fancied Michael was striding towards her. His face a
fleeting resemblance on some stranger.

Tears welled. She glimpsed the pucker of anxiety that Tod invoked
in the boy. Sad that her husband had been prouder of his first Mercedes
than his only son. Where are you, Mike? she thought. Please stay safe
and well.

Michael had been a difficult baby. Miserable with colic, disturbing
their sleep.

'Can't abide kids his age,' Tod groaned. 'Wait until the lad starts
kicking a football. Then I'll know what to do.'

But Michael hated rough and tumble sports.

She recalled his grubby, tear-stained face. 'Please, Mum. Please, don't
make me go.'

'If he doesn't like it, Tod…'

'Football will make a man of him. Stop snivelling, son. Get your
boots.'

Winters, Michael had suffered flare-ups of asthma.

The doctor advised, 'Have him refrain from boisterous games. They
appear to aggravate his condition.'

Reluctantly, Tod agreed. The attacks had markedly reduced.

Michael had blossomed at the preparatory school. Art gave him the
greatest pleasure. Detailed drawings brightened almost every page of
his workbooks. Teachers marvelled at his talent. Paintings revealed a
maturity beyond his years. The lad was only ten or eleven when he
began to win prizes.

Marta glimpsed a dreaming light in his eyes.

'Daddy, I want to be a painter when I grow up.'

Tod barely glanced at the work. 'A pity you don't show the same enthusiasm for sport.

A shadow crossed the boy's face.

'Lad, let me tell you something. I had to leave school at thirteen. People call me a self-made man. I'm giving you the opportunity to make something of yourself the easy way. Follow the money…'

'Daddy, I want to paint.'

'You'll grow up and forget such silly ideas.'

One of the teachers said, 'Talent like that… Your Michael could have a brilliant future in the artistic field.'

Tod moved him to a school acclaimed for their cadet unit and military graduates. Michael couldn't wait to leave.

Marta glimpsed Tod's Mercedes in the drive. Switched on the light. Glanced around the room. Adjusted magazines, ones that were already tidy. She dreaded the task ahead. How to break the news. Stubborn, yes: but surely Tod loved their son?

Her husband scowled. 'Lord, what a day. He handed her his bulging briefcase. Lowered his bulk into a leather chair. Massaged his neck.

Not even a token kiss, she thought. 'You…you're early. It's not even nine o'clock.'

'I've some figures to look over after dinner. Where's our layabout?'

She bit back anger. 'Are you referring to Michael?'

'Of course I mean Michael. Who else thinks the world owes him a living?'

'He's gone.'

'Out, you mean?

She gestured. 'There's a note.'

Marta saw his face whiten, then flush.

My life would be meaningless without Karen and my painting. Both are as necessary to me as breathing. Sorry if I've disappointed you. Mike.

'Painting? Love? Huh.'

Tod crumpled the note. Flung it towards the wastebasket. 'Let the pup find out what life's about. I starved through a depression. Built the company from nothing. He'll come crawling back when he runs out of dosh.'

'I've rung everyone…'

'Blast him. Worrying us like this. Let's have dinner. I've work to finish.'

Marta gagged at the every mouthful. Pushed her plate aside.

Tod raised his eyebrows. 'Not eating, luv? Don't let him worry you.'

The telephone shrilled.

Tod gave a start.

She rushed to answer, surging with hope. Let the phone crash into its receiver. 'A…a wrong number.' Marta shivered. Noted that Tod's food was almost untouched. A man who looked forward to every meal…

'I've no time for this.' He threw down his napkin. Strode down the corridor.

She heard the study door bang shut.

Marta ignored the gleaming dishwasher. Stacked everything in the sink. Needing to do something. Anything. Hot water bubbled into the detergent. She scoured every dish by hand. Rinsed, dried and stored them.

Oh, God, how can I bear it?

The evening ached with memories. Maybe a good show would do the trick? A cacophony of brutalised bodies and violence leapt from the screen. She pressed the off button.

Marta hesitated outside the study. Heard pacing within. Agonising, no doubt, over some business worry. Upstairs, a stranger stared from the gilt-edged mirror. Wide, frightened eyes. Indirect lighting revealed every line. She slipped into her embroidered nightgown. Brushed out long blonded hair. Turned back the Mexican flower patterned quilt. Determined not to cry.

Months passed. The disappearance had long vanished from the tabloids and TV. Part of a growing number of missing persons, young and old.

Not knowing whether Mike and Karen were dead or alive hurt the most.

A kindly Salvation Army officer took an interest in their case. 'Young people are often found when they're ready.'

Marta tensed at very knock on the door, or ring of the phone. The ache of loss never went away.

She lay still, feigning sleep. Untouched in the wasteland of a king-size bed. Sensing Tod's rigid posture. Mulling over business problems, no doubt, she thought. Cares more for work than his own son.

Tod edged closer. 'Awake, Marta?' A sadness tinged his voice. 'Can...can we talk?'

Surprised, she shrugged. 'Why not?' How cold and uncaring she sounded. Yet missing the old intimacy.

He switched on the light. 'I...I haven't done any work tonight. Can't concentrate. Called the police again...'

'Nothing? If...if only we knew he was safe.'

Tod stared off into the distance. 'I've done a lot of thinking lately. Recalled when Mike was a little chap. Wanted me to help him with a model aeroplane. I'd arranged to play golf that Sunday. Business associate. The disappointment on Mike's face haunts me still.'

'About money. As usual.'

He swallowed. 'Don't be like that, luv. I...I meant to make time for him. Suddenly, he didn't need me any more.' He sighed. 'At least I never tried to force him into the business like my poor old dad did with me...'

Marta gaped. 'What? Michael's "choice" was doing what you wanted.'

'So it's my fault he's gone?'

'Well, you...you did denigrate...'

'His bloody paintings. Where are all these masterpieces? Tell me that?'

Her eyes flashed. 'I've something to show you.' She shrugged into her dressing gown. Took a key from her jewel case.

The shrubbery twittered with starlings. She carried a bobbing flashlight past immaculate lawns. Not that Tod ever cut them. He rarely entered the garden any more.

Marta fumbled with the lock. 'Welcome to Michael's studio.'

Aeons had passed since Tod had glanced inside the old shed. A strong aroma of oil paint tickled his nostrils. Tod blinked in the sudden brilliance of light. His jaw dropped.

Every wall vibrated with brilliant works. A freshly completed canvas sat against an easel. Others were carefully stacked, row upon row of them.

He stood in front of one painting. Swirling among the angry reds and blacks, a vortex of grief and loss.

Prowled around the room. Once, twice. Whistled. 'So many. How could he leave this…this Aladdin's cave? Not that I'm any expert. But I never expected anything so…so…'

'Stunning?' She shivered. 'You never took the trouble to find out.'

Tod shook his head. 'They vibrate with such…such…power. I'm not sure if that's the way to describe it.' He shook his head. 'I feared he was wasting my allowance. Never guessed he's spent most here, on his work. Oh, why didn't he tell me?'

'When were you ever prepared to listen?'

His face grew sombre. 'Maybe you're right.'

'Mike was preparing for an exhibition.' Wait until she told Mike his father had actually referred to painting as 'work'.

God, where could that boy be?

Tod wiped his eyes. 'I'd become my own father. Closed my eyes to Michael's gift.' He slumped onto and old cane chair. 'Forgive me, Marta. For being so blind. But I did everything to ensure Michael had the comforts of life.'

'You tried to bully him into doing what you wanted.' For once, he must hear the truth.

Tod's shoulders sagged. 'Don't rub it in. I've only realised these past months… Without Michael, money means…nothing.'

She sighed. 'That blue painting…with the lonely figure… He

planned to enter that into the Young Artists National Painting Competition…this month.'

Tod gazed at the piece. 'That one grabbed my attention right away. Somehow, it makes me…'

'Sad? Me, too.'

'Oh, why would he leave all this?'

'After the way you raged at him?'

He groaned, 'Don't rub it in.' He moved closer. Put an arm around her trembling shoulders.

She felt cherished. The first time in years.

Tod wiped his eyes. 'Do you think Mike would mind if I came down here sometimes? I feel closer to my son than I've ever been.'

'I'm sure he'd feel – honoured.'

In taking stock of his life, Tod rekindled a kindness Marta hadn't glimpsed since early days. He returned home at a reasonable hour. 'I'm grooming Fenton to take over.'

Her eyes widened. 'An early retirement?'

'Why not? Let's take that world trip.'

'We talked of it so often.' Her face clouded. 'If only Mike…'

His jaw trembled. 'It's the not knowing that kills me too.'

They embraced. It felt so right.

One afternoon, the telephone jangled. Marta rushed in from the garden.

It was Tod. His words rose with excitement. 'H-have you seen the papers?'

Her surge of joy. 'It's Michael? They've found him?'

Silence. 'If only. B-but guess who's won the National Painting Competition?

She felt like weeping. 'Ted, please. Don't joke about such a thing.'

'I entered that painting. Mike had already signed the coupon. Do you reckon he'd be…?'

'Angry? I think not. If only…'

'…our lad was here? I fancy when Mike gets the good news, he'll be back.'

She allowed herself to hope. On a high for the first time since Michael left.

In the days to follow, her dreams evaporated. Came the night of the award. Still no Mike. Marta felt numb.

Karen's mother joined Tod and Marta. The women embraced. Sharing their fears without the need for words.

Tod accepted the award on behalf of Michael. Delivered a poignant speech. Many in the audience suffered unexpected colds. 'My son. The painter.' Tod's voice grew hoarse. He spoke about the generation gap. Left the rostrum. Thunderous applause.

He gave Marta the embossed certificate. 'We'll put the cheque in his account. I was so sure.' He stared around the departing crowd. Yet expecting Michael to step forward.

She shivered. Drew the cashmere evening wrap around her chilled shoulders. 'Let's go, darling.' How many years since she'd called him that?

They arrived home.

The insistent wail of the telephone echoed along the empty corridor. Marta felt like letting it ring. She had nothing left to say. 'Yes?' Her voice was cold. Distant.

'Hi, Mum.'

She flamed into life. 'Mike! It's Michael… Where are you?'

'Miles from anywhere. Fancy me winning the national award.'

Tod surged forward. 'Has Mike heard the news? Let me speak to him.'

Marta gestured wait. 'You've seen the TV?'

'No TV out here, Mum. We heard the winners' names on the radio. Thought, wow. That must be me. Thanks, Mum. Bet Dad isn't too pleased.'

'Oh, Michael. Darling, it was your father who entered the painting.'

'Dad? You've got to be kidding.'

Ted grabbed the phone. 'Congratulations, Mike. I'm so darned proud of you. I've been an old fool – forgive me. And come home, lad.'

'Thanks, Dad. But I am home: with Karen and our baby.'

'You're married? With a child?'

He laughed. 'Who needs a piece of paper? I love Karen. And yes, she's expecting. You were right, Dad. Art isn't everything. Sure, I still paint. But a group of us are healing a rundown farm. Planting native trees and vegetation. Koala habitat. We can really use that prize money.'

'Farming?' said Tod. 'There's no future in that. Now, with your talent...'

Marta shot him a glance.

Tod laughed. 'Come home for a visit, son. Bring Karen and the baby.'

Marta's eyes brimmed. 'Give me that phone. I must call Karen's mum.'

Belle of the Ball

A chatter of excitement soared in the Victoria Hotel change room. I relished the heady mixture of perfumes, fragrant as a tropical garden.

Mum chatted to one of the other women.

'We've made it,' Vivi whispered.

I giggled. 'Thanks to Poppy's magic.'

She nodded. 'Our fairy godmother.'

Other girls went out every week. We were lucky to make it once a month. Our cousin knew how desperate we felt for company and excitement.

She'd grinned. 'An isolated farm in the mountains is far from the ideal location for two girls with stars in their eyes. Not on dance night.' She'd winked. 'Leave it to me.'

Poppy took Mum aside. 'Walt and I are going to the Carnival Ball, Genn – what a shame you'll be missing out!'

Surprise, surprise! Mum could hardly wait.

Vivi giggled. 'Mission accomplished.'

Teenagers jostled for space at the foxed mirror. Donned bright nylon dresses with safe necklines. Supervised by doting mothers.

I wriggled my excitement. This would be only the second time I'd worn my gown. Daddy's surprise gift – and it hadn't even been my birthday. I kept it in a cocoon of tissue paper, soft beneath my fingers. A shiver. Scarcely able to believe the lovely turquoise blue organza strapless that awaited. I slipped it on.

Mum pursed her lips. She snapped. 'For goodness sakes, stand still while I zip you up.'

A pirouette around the room. A lovely swirl of that flared skirt against my legs. 'What do you think, Mum?'

'Stop showing off, will you?' She frowned. 'It's way too bare. Trust your father to buy you something expensive and unsuitable.' She held out the bolero. 'Put this on.'

'Mum, it's 1957. Not 1857.'

'That's all very well.' She pursed her lips again. 'For a girl of seventeen.'

I slipped into my new silver sandals.

My sister shot me a rueful glance. 'I might as well go home.'

'Don't be silly, sis. You look lovely.'

Against my better judgement, I shrugged into the bolero.

We walked across the moonlit fields. Waltz music drifted from the weatherboard hall. I breathed in the cool air, with a crazy urge to scoop up handfuls of stars, scattering them among the diamante on my pleated bodice. In the earthy aroma of petrichor, anything seemed possible.

Mum broke my reverie. 'For goodness sakes. Come along.'

Groups of young men clustered around the doorway. They cast amused eyes over the arriving talent.

We dreaded Mum sitting beside us. She made no secret of listening to potential partners' every word. Her glare was guaranteed to put off all but the most determined of them.

Cousin Poppy waved from across the room. Bless her, I thought.

'Poppy looks lonely, Mum. Why don't you join her?'

Mum shot me a look. 'But I thought... Oh, all right.' She left.

We giggled with relief.

The band struck up a quick step. On the stage, ruddy-faced graziers in moleskins and western shirts squeezed accordions. A red-haired spinster from the post office, all arms and chin, coaxed tunes from her fiddle.

It surprised me to see a former beau, Ivan. He clacked away with the bones.

I whispered, 'He hasn't noticed me yet.

Feet tapped to the music.

My sister danced off. Girls feigned exciting conversation. Faked smiles. Suppose no boys asked one to dance? I felt relieved that others felt nervous, too,

One by one, blossoms beside me waltzed off. I studied my brightly polished nails. The room grew warm. Off came my bolero. Probably the first strapless worn at Moonan Flat.

The temperature seemed to rise a notch or two. The very air sizzled with electricity. One boy whirled me away. Then a second. A third… Self-confidence soared.

The latest lad asked, 'How do you keep up your top?

'Magic. Isn't it obvious?'

He laughed. We shared a chuckle over scandalised glances from oldies.

A grin from my latest partner. 'Come with me to the movies on Saturday night, princess?'

'Sorry. We live miles away…' If only. Cursing my luck.

Ivan, my old flame, whirled me away. Grinning, he held me close. I felt a tinge of nostalgia.

'You're still my lovely girl.'

I blushed.

A stranger smiled. 'Shame there isn't a competition tonight. You'd be Belle of the Ball.'

Another number, a different boy. 'We're on a working holiday from New Zealand.' Matt told of snow-capped peaks, mirrored in pristine lakes. Of braided rivers. 'They surge across meadows of smooth stones in the spring melt.'

His friend, Ray, danced with Vivi. Regulars for the remaining hours.

Matt smiled. 'We'd love to take you home.'

Vivi glanced my way. 'Why not? We're staying the night with Poppy at Dry Creek.'

'We'll ask our parents.' I treasured this opportunity for a normal date. Driven home like any teenager.

We sought approval from Dad.

Ask your mother.'

She said, 'Ask Dad.'

I flashed a reassuring smile. 'We'll bring the boys to meet you.'

One dance melded into another. We delayed parental introductions. Reluctant to miss a moment of the fun.

Poppy confided later, 'Gossips had a field day over your dress. It worried your mother. Increasingly anxious, she said, "The girls were going to introduce those boys. Where are they?"' She had laughed. 'The night's young, Genn.'

The progressive barn dance. I found myself in Rick's arms. Months earlier, we'd clicked in a big way.

His eyes glowed with mingled shock and pleasure. 'Dessie! I didn't expect to see you here.'

Chemistry took my breath away. My sexy chuckle. 'You never know when I'll turn up.'

His lopsided grin. 'I can see that.'

Time to change partners. Rick held me seconds longer than necessary.

I recalled the last time we'd met. He'd begged me to attend the next dance. Dad scuttled my plans. Had the cheek to ask an uncle to teach me to dance. The old darling didn't leave my side all evening. I burnt with embarrassment and humiliation. Reluctant to hurt uncle's feelings. Not glancing to right or left the whole evening. I'd never know whether Rick turned up. Relieved to leave early, devastated by Daddy's ploy, I'd sobbed myself to sleep. A sudden insight. Suppose my father had bought my gown to atone for his guilt?

Matt and Ray joined us for supper. They marvelled at the gargantuan country feast. Home-made sponges, Lamingtons, scones, slices, apple pies… And who should be sitting directly opposite? Rick!

He had brought a girl from Scone. But glanced at Matt with an expression of pure jealousy.

Afterwards, the tempo of excitement sped up. The whirl and frenzy of flying feet. All too soon, the music died. I stood chuckling and breathless. Dizzy with exultation.

Matt wiped his brow. 'Wow! What an evening.'

Parents collected drowsy children from the sleeping annex. One little lad grabbed balloons. Entangled in paper streamers.

We introduced the boys to our anxious parents. 'Matthew, Raymond.'

Dad towered above us, grim-faced. Arms crossed, voice glacial. 'What are your second names?' His interrogation went on and on.

Increasingly embarrassed, I craved friendly chit-chat. Discussion of their experiences in Australia. An invitation to visit the farm…

At last, Dad ran out of steam. 'Very well. You may drive the girls home.'

His caveat? A convoy. Mum and Dad in the leading vehicle, us in the middle. Poppy and Walt's car bringing up the rear.

I couldn't believe it. The boys were equally gobsmacked.

Strolling towards the car, a familiar voice shouted derogatory remarks to the Kiwis. They feigned deafness. We drove off. At that moment, I glimpsed Rick, illuminated by our headlights. What had possessed him?

Our departure became the talk of the town.

One of the locals, drove past, yelling, 'Good on yer, Kiwis.'

Matt gave a triumphant blast on the horn.

A friendly goodnight kiss, before the boys drove off. Luckily, they didn't accept our invitation to coffee.

Next day Poppy told us, 'Your Dad told Walt, "If they don't drive straight back, I'll investigate."'

Poppy laughed with me over Rick's odd behaviour. 'Just quietly, I think he's jealous.'

Beware of the Cat

The ward chattered. Wheels squeaked on the linoleum tiles, crockery rattled.

Behind the bed curtain, Laura Bentham breathed in the aroma of freshly brewed tea. Mmm. That smells good… She glimpsed a movement of aqua uniform.

'Tea for you, Mrs Bentham? I'll leave yours right here, on Mrs Owen's bed table.'

'Thanks. I'll only be a minute.' Laura slipped into a nightie, packing away her day clothes. Admitted for vein surgery, she recalled the reaction of her friend, Helen, to news of her op.

'Sheer vanity.'

'Not at all.' Laura had chuckled. 'Cosmetic issues aside, my surgeon says varicose veins damage other vessels. And surgery will relieve the ache of tired legs too.'

Helen shrugged. 'Maybe it's for the best, then.'

Laura swished back the screens.

Her silver-haired neighbour said, 'I'm recuperating after a cataract operation.' Adding, 'I'm expecting my daughter, Ruby.' A great sigh. 'She means well.'

At that moment, a weather-beaten face strode Mrs Owen's way. Lurid pink towelling tracksuit, trainers. Grim expression. Ruby pecked her mother on the cheek, gave Laura a polite nod.

'Oh, look, Mum,' Ruby said, face transformed by a smile. 'Isn't that kind of the staff? They've left me a tea.' She grabbed the cup and downed the lot. 'I really needed that.'

Laura's jaw dropped. By then, the refreshments trolley wasn't even a teapot on the horizon. She made do with a lukewarm glass of water.

The interloper munched her biscuit.

She watched Ruby ferret around on her mother's locker. A woman on the lookout for trouble, Laura mused.

'Have you had your eye drops, Mum?'

The old lady hesitated. 'I'm not sure, dear.'

Ruby accosted one of the nurses. 'Has my mother received her eye drops?'

The nursed checked Mrs Owens chart. 'Ya, ya. Says so here.'

Her accent and blonde hair made Laura think she was Dutch.

The nurse hurried away.

Ruby sniffed. 'I don't believe her. Doesn't even speak proper English. Where do they find them?'

A veiled uniform sped up the ward.

Ruby sprang to her feet. 'Excuse me. Has Mum received her eye drops?'

The nurse glanced at Mrs Owen's chart. 'Yes, she has.' The RN departed.

Ruby scowled. 'My goodness. It's no use trying to argue with them. You've never received the right drops since admission.'

The old lady blinked. 'Oh, dear. Haven't I? Are you sure?'

'Who's sure of anything around here?'

Lunch. Ruby hovered over her mother's tray. Tut-tutted. 'Mum, wipe your mouth. You're drooling. Don't use your fork like that…'

Laura thought, heaven save me from a finicky daughter.

The old lady gagged over the pureed food. 'I've had enough, luv.'

'Just a couple more spoonfuls, Mum.'

'Can't dear. I'll be sick.'

Ruby looked annoyed. 'Oh, have it your way. If you don't want to get well, what can I do?'

Laura bit her lip. For Pete's sake, she thought. Give your mother a break.

Without another word, Ruby grabbed her bag and stalked off.

Mrs Owens sighed. 'Just wish she wouldn't fuss.'

Laura gave a sympathetic smile. 'What do they say? The road to hell…'

Another patient chuckled. 'Paved with good intentions?'

They all laughed.

Operation day dawned. Nil by mouth from midnight, Laura's surgery would take place early afternoon. She struggled to ignore the heavenly aroma of bacon, eggs and toast. Recuperating patients tucked into breakfast. Cutlery clinked, plates rattled.

Laura saw a tall, wizened lady hobble into the ward. She clutched the knob of an ornate walking stick.

The newcomer glimpsed a medico writing up notes. Her voice resonated from one end of the room to the other. 'When is my operation, doctor?'

The anaesthetist grinned. 'What's your name?'

'Goldfarb. Sarah Goldfarb.'

'Let me see. You're last on the list.'

'Last on the list? I don't believe this. I haf come on two buses and it's barely seven o'clock and you haf told me I'm last on the list?'

'That's right. Yours is only a comparatively small operation. The others are major surgery. Theirs take time.'

'I haf to speak to someone in charge. There must be something to be done. I haf not had anything to eat. What time will my operation be?'

He shrugged. 'Two or three p.m.'

'You want that I should wait until two or three p.m. after getting here at this hour? I must speak to someone. Why can't I be done first? Tell me that? Why must I wait when I was here first?'

The rant went on and on. The other patients exchanged glances. Stifled giggles. Within minutes, Sarah was moved to the top of the list. The wardsman wheeled her away to theatre, still complaining.

'I've torn my shoulder ligament. Stood on a small glass table. Broke under my weight.'

With Sarah out of earshot, the ward exploded in mirth.

'So that's how it's done,' said Laura.

'My, oh my,' said Mrs Owens. 'What a to-do.'

'But it worked,' said the blonde with crutches. 'Must try it sometime.'

They laughed some more.

The creak of a gurney announced Sarah's return. Her moans resonated throughout the ward. Over and over, she called for a pan. 'I'm sorry but I must go. I cannot help it.'

Nurses rushed to and fro, red-faced and perspiring from attending to her needs. Patients raised eyebrows, exchanged glances.

Laura left for her surgery. Grateful to have a break from the noise. On her return, she blinked awake. Legs swathed in crêpe bandages.

'You all right, dear?' asked Mrs Owens.

'I...I think so. Gosh, someone's in a bad way.'

'It's Sarah. Her moans haven't stopped since you left, poor thing.'

'All afternoon? Surely they gave her pain relief?'

A chorus of voices. 'She's refused it. Several times.'

Evening. The head nurse looked grim. She approached Sarah's bed with a kidney tray, syringe and determined expression. 'Doctor wants you to have something for your pain. It will help you sleep.'

'Help me sleep? I haf never taken anything for sleep in my life.'

'Nevertheless, we think you should have this tonight. Just a little injection for the pain.'

Blissful silence. A collective sigh of relief.

The following morning, a visitor arrived. Skin baked the colour of an old leather suitcase. The odd expression in his eyes set Laura wondering.

Sarah introduced him as her forty-something son.

'I'm the oldest surfie in Clovelly.' His boasts crashed and eddied around the room. 'Most are in their teens. Beat them all. Why, only the other day...'

He failed to ask how Sarah was feeling. Laura felt surprised.

The son cackled. 'You should have brought me a cake before you came to hospital, Mother. It would help me to surf. Soon you'll be well. Then you'll surf better than me.'

Laura and Mrs Owens shared a takes-all-types glance.

Sarah looked sombre. 'I just vomited before you came.'

A sardonic laugh. 'It's only the effects of the anaesthetic.'

Next moment, Sarah sat up and spewed into a bowl.

He cackled. 'You sit very well.'

'Excuse me for vomiting in front of you.' She wiped her mouth. 'It's terrible. And I need a bedpan every ten minutes.'

A nurse bore the bowl away.

He fell about laughing. 'The indignity of a hospital. Oh, by the way, the cat's better. If it interests you.'

'Not really.'

'The cat you love.' He sniggered. 'Told me it will bite you again when you come to my house.'

Sarah looked bleak.

'Seen the doctor?'

'Once.'

'He will visit you again tomorrow. And, no doubt, charge you, even for the visits he hasn't made. Ha, ha, ha...'

Mrs Owens whispered, 'Let's hope the jolly cat bites him.'

'Indeed.' Laura chuckled. 'He makes your Ruby seem like an angel.'

Paradise

Derek gazed in wonderment at the tiny island. Set like an emerald in turquoise water, and reflected by the mirrored surface of the lake. It shimmered in the morning light. Delineated, suddenly, by a wisp of rainbow. Gone in seconds. As a kid, I dreamed of visiting such a place, he thought.

A skiff reclined nearby. Oars at the ready, he thought, with a wry grin. What harm would it do if I borrowed it for a while, maybe an hour or two at most? A mad, lovely idea. Something he normally wouldn't contemplate.

The sun rose towards its zenith. Shouting, seize the day.

He peered through his spectacles. Excitement on the rise, edged by foliage and sand. Who knew what exotic flowers, birds and animals might await his discovery? A siren song of adventure and magic urged him not to wait.

Derek resumed his walk. His orange sneakers crunched in the sand. He kept glancing across the bay. A perfect day, with just a hint of crispness from snow on the distant mountains.

How wonderful to be away from that wretched American woman and her husband, he thought. They had taken a special interest in him on this trip.

The loud colours of Howard's shirts matched her voice. 'We've been around the world eighteen times. Ain't that right, Howie?'

'Sure is, honey. And you say this is your first trip out of Australia?'

Derek blushed. 'Well, yes. But next year I'm off to Europe.'

'Land sakes. Did you hear that, Howie? The first time like our...' She never did finish her sentence. Wiped her eyes.

Leaving him at a loss. What did I say, he wondered.

At breakfast, Derek had used the excuse of a sore throat to remain at the hotel. The others straggled away to visit yet another museum of indigenous relics. During the last ten days on the tourist coach, he thought, I've seen enough musty bones. In and out of collections.

Derek eyed the brilliant sunshine pouring through his hotel window, overjoyed. 'The mist's evaporated.'

Slipping into jeans, navy-blue T-shirt and orange sneakers, he hurried outside. How much better he felt, being on his own. Breathing in the air, tangy with saline and pine. Beautiful. It must be lovely out on the water, he mused. Haven't rowed in years.

He strode on. An inner voice teased, C'mon, what's keeping you? Derek cursed his middle-class morality. Always doing the right and proper thing.

He glanced back. The boat beckoned. Every sturdy line of its timbers mocked him. For once, he'd do something wild and daring. After all, he reasoned, borrowing isn't stealing. I'll find the owner. More than happy to pay the cost of hire.

A single cloud floated above. He dared not linger.

Derek set off at a run. Keen to depart before courage deserted him. Noticing the boat's name, he grinned. *Paradise*. Appropriate, for such a lovely spot.

The small craft proved easy to manoeuvre into the water. Derek took no heed of the life jacket. Once seated, he adjusted the rowlocks. Lifted the oars. Fell easily into the old rhythm. All I need, to make my day complete, is some pretty companion, he mused. Maybe on the island? Derek chuckled.

I'll take some photographs to show Mum and my sister. Pattie would love to see where I've been. Luckily, I've my new camera. Darn, what an idiot: he'd left the Nikon on his bed. No matter; this would be the perfect chance to look around. Should it reach his expectations, he'd be back.

The island pulled him nearer. At the same time, it seemed to push him away. Tantalisingly attainable one minute, impossible to reach the next. It puzzled him. Was this a sort of mirage? For some reason, it seemed no closer, though he had rowed for at least half an hour.

He glanced towards his wrist. Only the pale imprint of a band against the golden tan. Blond hairs stood up: the day had grown chilly. Mother would have reminded him to bring a coat. Bless her.

He had a vison of Mother and his sister, Pattie, at the airport. They hugged him goodbye, as if forever. A silence had fallen.

'Have you packed clean hankies?' asked his mother, just as she used to when he set off for school.

The silly question hung between them. Derek flushed.

'Mum! Stop fussing.' Pattie hugged him. Turning aside to hide the tears from her kid brother.

He chuckled. 'Lighten up, girls. I'm visiting the North Island of New Zealand, not the North Pole.'

The last call for his flight.

'Must go.'

A final embrace. He'd shouldered his backpack. Given a jaunty wave. Joined other passengers in Departures.

Could it only be forty minutes, give or take, since he left the shore? It felt an eternity. He pondered that strange thing called time. Some moments stretched like elastic. Others, sped by. 'And still I struggle to reach this forsaken place,' he muttered. Like in a dream. Would he ever make it?

Far beyond him, the water surface shivered. Reflections broke up into a thousand fragments of shattered glass. The boat shuddered, caught by a gust of freezing wind. Derek's teeth chittered.

Low clouds roiled on by, blotting out the sun. Lightning flashed. Thunder rolled and growled. The island hid behind a misting shroud of white. Stung by sleet and drops of bitter rain, Derek made to head for shore. Struggling to gauge the direction.

The boat leapt every which way. Derek was soaked to the skin, blinded by the surge of waves. Spinning in a whirlpool of howling wind.

Up to his calves in water, he fought on. A wave of petrifying ferocity swamped the tiny craft. Flinging him into icy water.

This is it, he thought. Disbelief. Grief. Oh, why didn't I wear that life jacket?

Glasses gone. Sneakers gone. And, at any moment, I'll be gone.

When did horror become tranquillity? Derek sped faster and faster towards a great white light. Engulfed by warmth and love.

That evening, Derek failed to appear at dinner.

Elspeth, the fat American woman, felt anxious. 'Should I get staff to fetch him something?'

Howie shrugged. 'He's young and strong. Sleep fits him like a glove. Do him more good than food.'

On their way to bed, Elspeth knocked on Derek's door. No response. 'Asleep, poor lamb. You're right, Howie. He needs his rest.'

Next morning, the sun blazed from cloudless blue.

'A welcome sight after yesterday's downpour,' Howie said.

The gale had uprooted trees, blown off roofs. Search and rescue busied themselves cleaning up the mess.

At breakfast, Elspeth glanced around. Alarmed at Derek's absence. 'Where can he be?'

Howie put down his paper. 'You're right, honey. It isn't like a healthy young man to skip two meals in a row. Sore throat or not.'

Elspeth raised the alarm. 'It's probably nothing but...'

The maid found Derek's bed unslept in. One of the staff recalled that, yesterday, Derek had left for a mid-morning hike. Not seen since.

Police set out in force, carrying out a search of walking trails. The whop, whop, whop of helicopters vibrated overhead. Scanning for the missing man.

Officers assembled on the beach. Elspeth and Howie huddled among their group. A chatter of shock and disbelief rose above the gentle lap of water.

Remnants and a few timber planks had been flung ashore among seaweed and other debris. Stark reminder of the transience of life. Testament to the force of the tempest.

A bystander shook his head. 'Once a boat.'

Police found a board with its name. '*Paradise*. Boat reported missing yesterday.' Could the disappearance and wreckage be linked?

About then, a young constable held up an orange sneaker, retrieved from among shells, sea grass and wreckage. 'Anybody recognise this?'

Elspeth gasped. 'My God! Officer, it's Derek's! He wore a pair just like that at breakfast. Yesterday morning.'

Howie nodded. 'You're right. I noticed them, too.'

'Name?' The constable took her statement. 'You'll be a witness at the inquest.'

She trembled. 'If only Derek had stayed at the hotel. Gargled his throat. I can't understand why he'd be out in a boat.'

'Why not?' A silver-haired bystander shrugged. 'Perfect day for a row. Wouldn't have known how quickly storms blow up in these parts.'

Howie frowned. 'Strange, there's no sign of...'

'The lad's remains?' Protruding teeth and thick glasses, a local, shook her head. 'Water's deep and cold hereabouts. A body just sinks to the bottom. Stays there forever.'

Elspeth gave a strangled cry. 'Oh, God, no...'

Howie put an arm around her shoulders. 'Let's go, darling. Nothing we can do here.'

Back at their five-star hotel, Elspeth gripped her cocktail. A plump, bejewelled hand. She couldn't stop shaking. 'His mother and sister arrive next week. For the inquest. I'll h-help if I can. Anything to...to make it easier.'

Opening her scuffed leather handbag, she drew out a yellowed photograph. A blond youth stared back. 'Derek was the same age as our... Odd both of them taken on their first...' She wiped swollen eyes. 'I know what it's like.'

They embraced.

'Yes, honey. We know what it's like.'

Coup de Foudre

Love at first sight. I drowned in those gorgeous blue eyes. Ached to hold her lithe body in my arms. To stroke that cream hair. But she flounced on her way. No casual pick-ups for this young lady, I thought. In sunny weather, she slipped by almost every day. I treasured her occasional haughty glance. She wasn't mine to claim, let alone to name. Laughing at my temerity, I dubbed her Samantha. As usual, she stalked off, without a sign that she had noticed my existence.

Samantha, I thought. Bliss of my heart. Enchantress of dreams. Every glimpse left me with a feeling of warmth. She might not be mine but I longed for the unthinkable – a cuddle. Only time would tell, and, so far, touch had proved elusive.

For several days in a row, Samantha failed to appear. I moped. Was she all right? Where might she be? Where did she live? That evening, I sat, deep in thought. Suppose we never met again?

My husband, Neville, gave me a long look. 'This has been going on far too long. Who is he?'

I groaned. 'Not he, she.' If only I'd had a camera to record the expression on his face. I laughed. 'It isn't what you think. I have been meeting someone. But not a lover.'

That Saturday morning, Samantha sat in the sun outside a neighbour's house. Licking her paws.

Neville whistled. 'Gosh, a Siamese! Isn't she lovely. Why didn't you tell me?'

'When do you ever listen?' I shrugged. 'Anyway, I've dubbed her Samantha. And, like Circe, the goddess, I hope her love for a family of choice is greater than for her family of origin.'

'Catnapping now, is it?'

'No! But should she choose to move house…'

He sniggered. 'Sounds like wishful thinking to me. She's never even let you pat her.'

'Not until meow. I mean now.'

Neville went on, 'Sleek and well-fed. Samantha must have a place of her own.'

I sighed. 'For someone with a fixed abode, she wanders a lot. Maybe she isn't happy at home?'

He grinned. 'I wouldn't count on it.'

Still. The thought gave me a slender thread of hope.

Tantalising glimpses went on. By then, Neville seemed cativated, too. But Samantha kept us out of paw's reach.

Another meeting. 'Hello, sweetie. I'm trustworthy…'

She strolled off on her aristocratic way.

Days went by without another sighting. I feared for Samantha's well-being.

Neville drove home from work. Anxiously put down his briefcase. 'Have you spotted Samantha?'

'Not so much as a whisker.'

He frowned. 'Odd that you've not seen her around. But she does belong elsewhere.'

I bit my lip. How could one be practical with the heart involved?

In the golden glow of evening, Samantha took her gamble. She crept closer. Ever closer. I hardly dared to breathe. She rubbed her cream body against my legs. The earth shook. Lightning flashed. I caressed her head. Ran my hand from her dusky, pointed ears, along the soft fur of her back, to the dark tip of her tail.

That night, my dream became reality: Samantha moved in. A fur coat her only luggage. The family took turns to nurse her. She made an inspection of our house. Not quite up to her standards, I suspect, but adequate under the circumstances. It wasn't long before my favourite chair became hers. I was allowed to sit there with her on my lap.

Our new friend deigned to sample the cuisine. Purred over breast of chicken. We discovered later that lesser flesh, or mince, brought a disdainful shake of a rear paw.

Next morning, Neville looked up from his breakfast of toast and honey. 'You're not cooking filet steak for that darned cat?'

I must have looked guilty. 'Only one small piece.'

He muttered something about special treatment.

Puss continued her forays into households along the street. Once, I spied her in a neighbour's house: she had the grace to look guilty.

Strangely, nobody ever claimed ownership.

Sometimes, we found ourselves creeping around on tiptoe. Not inclined to disturb a sleeping Samantha. She held an upper arm and paw across her eyes, to shut out the light.

Her domain extended to the highest ramparts of our suburban castle. At least once a day, she climbed onto the garage, leapt across to the house roof, peered under eaves and into chimneys. Inspection complete, she descended, often in a heart-stopping leap to the ground.

On humid nights, Samantha insisted on a place at the foot of our bed. Eyes closed, she lifted her face towards the air con. The breeze riffled her whiskers. We chuckled at her blissful expression.

Our friend refused the indignity of a flea collar. One whiff of the insecticide and she vanished for hours. But she did brave the summer ritual of regular hygiene. Immersed in a baby's bath, she underwent a shampoo and rinse.

A preliminary rub dry and I draped a fresh towel across my knees. Samantha tucked her head under my armpit, as if she couldn't bear the indignity of the ordeal to follow: a hunt and kill of fleas. Legs drawn up against her stomach, hoarse cries warned me to take care.

Tweezers probed for those dark and pesky vampires. Five, six. Splat! Another…Ten, twenty… Over at last… She shook all over, displaying her disgust. Curled up in the sun to sleep off the nightmare.

Windy days saw her kick up her paws and rocket around the house. Playing hide-and-seek with my daughter, Naomi. And Cedric, my son, tossed paper balls into the air for her to catch in her mouth. Moments like those, she made to sharpen her claws on the furniture.

A shout, 'Stop.'

We rushed to intervene. She fled the scene.

I liked it when she sat on a windowsill, an Egyptian sphinx, observing the passing throng. Disdainful of human contact. But Samantha invariably demanded a daily dose of human love from her chosen family. Springing onto the nearest lap and purring contentedly.

One day, puss leapt over the fence. A protruding nail tore soft skin. She padded into the house, going to every guest in the lounge room. Tail held high, she showed the injury, near her bottom. Gave vociferous and prolonged voice to her outrage.

Samantha hated to be ignored. With cries of make way for me, she batted aside the obstruction with her head, whether it be homework, manuscript or magazine. Making space enough to settle into a comfortable position.

She appointed herself site manager of any outside project. Peering into holes and jumping over bricks. Seemed to have the idea that feline approval was necessary. Shoddy work? She'd meow her disapproval.

Samantha took breakfast on the dot of six a.m. One morning, at half-past eight, she yowled from hunger. Disgusted to find me lounging in bed. I ignored her pleas for a while She delivered a warning nip on the arm. Not only surprised but offended, I feigned tears. She gave me a 'you've got to be kidding' glance, followed by a second nip.

Guess who received prompt service?

She made clear her aversion to certain pop music. If one of my kids sang 'Muskrat Love', regarded by some as among the worst music of the seventies, she gave the singer a warning nip. And once, my son hurt his toe. My husband tried to soothe five-year-old Cedric's tears. Samantha must have figured Neville had inflicted the injury. She gave a toothy rebuke, not breaking the skin.

A recurring dream kept Neville awake. Vivid images of Samantha at bay on some sort of blue mountain, eyes ablaze. Below, two assailants, a tabby and a marmalade cat, spat and snarled. I must be going crazy he thought; that darned cat is even disturbing my sleep. Unable to drift off, he wondered, did Samantha come inside last night? Best check her rug. Oops! Not there. He clicked on the outside light. His jaw dropped.

In the drive outside, two tomcats, of the same colouring and clawing postures as in his dream, met Neville's astonished gaze. Samantha had backed up on top of the car. Her eyes glowed, stop lights of fear and fury. Fur fluffed up to twice her size.

'Scram, you mongrels,' he shouted. Neville cradled her in his arms. 'It's okay, sweetie.'

Gratitude? Samantha voiced the full blast of her displeasure, having expected a prompt response to her distress signal.

About the Author

Decima Wraxall, née Wright, was born in Newcastle, NSW, Australia. She spent her early years in the Alpine region of the Upper Hunter Valley. A graduate from RPA Hospital, Sydney, Decima worked as an RN for over thirty years.

Her fascination for the French language resulted in a diploma, accredited by the Alliance Française de Paris and the French Ministry of National Education. She spent a month honing her skills at ELFCA Institute and was a paying guest of a French family at Hyères, in the South of France.

Since raising her two children, Decima has embarked on another lifetime passion – the written word. Her fictional memoir *Black Stockings, White Veil, A tale of Adversity, Triumph and Romance,* was a finalist in the 2009 New Generation Indie Book Awards, for Historical Fiction.

She has co-edited two anthologies: *Our Womens' Work*, a finalist in the 2014 New Generation Indie Book Awards for women's issues, and *Bare*. Decima has received prizes for poetry and short stories.

Recent successes include the publication of three poetry collections, *Bloom, Flame* and *The Mists of Time*, in addition to a coming-of-age novel *Stolen Fruit* – all published by Ginninderra Press, thanks to the splendid endeavours of Brenda and Stephen Matthews.